Wet Matches:
A Novel

Randolph Randy Camp

ISBN: 1466389281
ISBN 13: 9781466389281

Dedicated to those who've been in the well.

-Randolph Camp

Table of Contents

CHAPTER ONE

Jack and Crystal

It seems that those who reach down and pull others out of the well, most often, are those who've been down in the well themselves. When Jack Canaday was twelve years old he was once in the well. The year was 1979. In the boys' bathroom at Jack's middle school an incident happened that changed his life forever. The thin six-grader nonchalantly walks in to take a leak. Jack's skinny arms lower his schoolbooks upon the edge of the sink as he migrates toward the middle urinal. Positioned in front of the urinal, Jack unzips his pants. A short hairbrush handle protrudes from Jack's back pocket. BAM! The door flies open! A small gang of Black bullies burst in! They're four stocky, menacing-looking seven-graders. Nervously, Jack stiffens his posture. Immediately, the beefy foursome surrounds

Jack at the urinal. Jack can't budge as the bullies' noses breathe hot air upon his neck. There's an awkward silence as Jack inconspicuously zips up his pants and tries to step away from the urinal. Jack's left shoulder is quickly blocked by a firm chest. One of the bullies asks, "Where ya' goin', white boy?" Jack doesn't respond. He swallows his tongue as fear invades his whole body. Another bully asks, "Got some money, white boy?" Not waiting for an answer, the bully's hand hastily searches Jack's front pants pockets. Jack inhales a huge gulp of air then bravely bulldozes the bully's chest with all of his might! The big seven-grader tumbles to the floor! Jack makes a dash towards his schoolbooks balancing on the edge of the sink but doesn't quite make it. The small-bodied six-grader is rushed, gang-tackled and wrestled to the floor! One of the thugs yanks Jack's hairbrush out of his back pocket Rising quickly from the floor with vengeance in his eyes, the alpha thug slam dunks Jack's schoolbooks into the trash can! The bully edges on the others, "Com'on, get 'em! Get 'em!"

Jack's twiggy legs are kicking wildly in all directions as the rowdy foursome manhandles and easily drags him across the floor into the nearest stall! Inside the crowded stall, Jack cries out, "Leave me alone!" A black hand rapidly covers Jack's mouth as muffled cries are faintly heard. As one of the bullies directs, "Pull his pants down!" the thug holding the hairbrush quickly positions himself near Jack's backside. Jack's shoes are wildly banging against the stall walls as the raunchy bullies yank his pants and underwear down, exposing his pale buttocks! The evil-eyed thug strategically flips the hairbrush to expose its short handle then commands, "Spread his legs! Spread 'em!" Easily, the young bullies gain control over Jack's frantically kicking legs as the black hand cupping his mouth tightens its grip! The short hairbrush handle slowly vanishes between Jack's white buttocks as a loud, muffled groan fills the air.

∽

It's twenty-one years later. Steady ocean waves rush the sandy shore as beach goers enjoy the California sun. Pedestrians stroll along the lengthy, wooden pier as graceful seagulls hover above. Several beach bars line the coast advertising their happy hours and open mike nights on colorful sandwich boards. Further inland, lofty lollipop palm trees border the streets of cozy and alluring Seaside, California. Home building has become a very lucrative business in this post card town. Along a developing cul-de-sac, a construction crew wearing hard hats labeled 'CCP' is busy hammering and erecting two-by-fours for the frames of three up-and-coming homes on separate lots. A magnetic sign on the door of a small office trailer boasts...

CCP
CANADAY CONSTRUCTION PROPERTIES
SEASIDE CALIFORNIA

A shiny, red Toyota Pathfinder pulls into the developing cul-de-sac, joining the rest of the crew's SUVs and pickups parked curbside. Stepping out of the glossy Pathfinder is thirty-three year old Jack Canaday, now a wealthy self made man who proudly shows off his tall, well-toned body in t-shirt and jeans. Walking towards the construction site's office trailer, Jack's proud face suddenly turns puzzled as he eyes a timid-looking Black boy hammering a nail into a two-by-four at the far-left lot. Jack's face reddens and tightens as he hurriedly steps toward the Black teen. Jack's eyes zero in on the teen's hammering technique while sternly standing over the boy's shoulder. Jack tightens his mouth then sighs in frustration. Unable to contain his bubbling angst, Jack loudly scorns at the shy-looking teen, "Who are you and why are you using those kinda' nails?" Before the boy has a chance to respond, Jack turns away then huffs and puffs toward the office trailer. Disappointed in himself, the Black teen sighs then lowers his head in shame. Along his way to the office trailer, Jack makes eye contact with one of his carpenters getting a drink of water from a nearby cooler. Jack tells the carpenter, "Make sure the kid use the right nails." And then Jack asks, "Is Donny here yet?" The carpenter promptly responds, "No problem, Mr. Canaday...Yep, Donny's in the office, Boss." Jack continues toward the trailer as the carpenter walks over to the humble teen and politely shows him the proper nails to use on the two-by-fours.

The tiny office trailer is clustered with rolled and unrolled blueprints scattered across atop the two desks and on the floor. A wall clock shows One o'clock. The right-corner desk is occupied by Jack's right-hand man, Donny, who's studying a stretched-out blueprint. Jack enters as Donny greets him with a touch of surprise, "Hey Jack, what-cha' doin' here? You and Crystal-" Slapping his forehead for forgetting, Jack interrupts, "Aw shit! That's right, the clinic!" And then he asks, "Donny, who's the Black kid out there?"

Donny gives Jack a look then explains, "That's Kevin Morris. He's the one from the High School Summer Job Hire Program. Remember we talked about boosting your PR, Jack? Is there a problem, Boss?" For the past twenty-one years, Jack has suppressed his distaste of Black men and it seems that he's still unable to face it head on. Jack sighs and somewhat nervously hand-brushes his hair to avoid Donny's question then awkwardly responds with, "No problem. He looks like a good kid...Hey, I better get to the clinic before Crystal has a fit...See ya, Donny." Getting back to the blueprint, Donny grins then utters, "Talk to ya' later, Boss."

Minutes later, Jack's red Toyota Pathfinder speedily pulls into the nearly-full parking lot in front of a red brick, one-story building fronted with the bold, black letters, DEPARTMENT OF HEALTH SERVICES. A small group of homeless men are standing near the front entrance. Their beat-up shopping carts of recyclable aluminum cans and dirty beer bottles are parked nearby. Jack avoids eye contact with the homeless men as he hurriedly walks toward the entrance door. One of the homeless men steps out of the group to get Jack's attention. He's a shirtless, Black man with unkept hair and soiled jeans. He brings his right hand upward to his mouth then gestures his mouth and fingers as if he's puffing a cigarette. Seeing that Jack isn't catching his drift, the Black homeless man asks, "Yo' bro, gotta' cigarette?" Jack doesn't respond. He never made eye contact. Jack's about to enter the clinic. The homeless man shoots Jack a bit of sarcasm, "Have a nice day, brother." Completely ignoring the homeless man, Jack opens the door and enters the clinic.

In the cramped lobby there aren't enough chairs for the weary crowd waiting for their names to be called. Reluctantly, some in the lobby are leaning against the walls. By the hungry, desperate look on the numerous faces in the waiting room it's obvious that this County Health clinic is their last chance of hope.

Colorful posters offering messages about drug prevention, HIV/AIDS prevention, pregnancy prevention and pre-natal care ornament the lobby walls. Clearly overworked, the receptionist looks frustrated while checking the names on the sign-in register and scanning the pile of intake questionnaire sheets atop the desk counter. A male intake worker emerges from a lengthy corridor cradling a client's folder. The intake worker calls out the next client, "James? Michelle James?" A pregnant Ms. James struggles out of her chair. Instantly, the empty chair is occupied again. The intake worker escorts penguin-walking Ms. James down the long corridor. Jack enters the lobby. The wall clock displays, '1:15'. Jack's contorted face says it well...that he'd rather be elsewhere. The receptionist spots Jack and notices his discomfort. She tries to lift his spirit, "Smile, Jack. Can't be that bad. You're late, you know. Crystal keep asking me if you'd come in yet. She's gotta client in intake. She'll be out in a few minutes...I would offer you a seat but you know the story here." Through the corner of his eyes, Jack glances at the colorful array of homeless and low-income adults along with wearisome teens cramped in the waiting room.

Jack tries to conceal his distaste with a forced smile at the tiresome receptionist as he responds with, "Thanks. I'll just stand here and look at your pretty face for a few minutes."

"Ooooo, wait 'til I tell Crystal you was hittin' on me", the playful receptionist responds. Down the corridor the doors are labeled 'INTAKE 1', 'INTAKE 2' and 'INTAKE 3.' Behind Door 2 is a small office of bare walls. Jack's wife, intake counselor Crystal Canaday, is planted behind a narrow desk attentively listening to an unkept, middle-aged homeless man seated opposite her in a plain, metal foldout chair.

Draped in soiled clothes, the homeless man's dirty, bare feet are dispensing an irritating odor. Inconspicuously, Crystal squints her eyes and twitches her nose while giving her client her undivided attention. The homeless man stutters, "I tr..tr..tri..tried loo..look..lookin' fo' ss..ss..some sh.. sh..shoes but ain..ain't nobody gg..gg..got none. Mm..mm.. my feet's hurtin' re..re.. real ba..ba..bad." Abruptly, Crystal bends over to untie the strings of her cushy nurse shoes then steps around the desk to size up her feet with her shoeless client.

Placing her left shoe next to the man's crusty right foot, Crystal's face beams with a big country smile. Speaking with a slight hint of a Southern drawl, Crystal offers, "Today's your lucky day." The humble man is taken aback as Crystal peels off her comfortable shoes and extends them to him. Overwhelmed by Crystal's compassion, a tear begins to streak down the homeless man's crusty face as he stutters, "Th. .th. .thank ya." Crystal nods pleasingly with, "You're very welcome, Sir."

Meanwhile, out in the waiting room, Jack is leaning against the counter as the receptionist shuffles through intake questionnaire sheets. Jack's face suddenly turns puzzled as he eyes his barefooted wife emerging from the corridor into the lobby with her client, who is now beaming proudly in his new nurse shoes.

After a warm embrace and a quick hello kiss, Crystal notices Jack eying her bare feet with a curious grin. Crystal smiles and says, "Just another day at the shop, Jack." There's a slight pause. Crystal isn't letting her husband off the hook that easy. She continues, "Where were you? Nancy's doing us a favor. I told you to be here at one." The receptionist smiles in amusement at the nearby conversation. Jack doesn't know how to answer his wife's question then he desperately utters, "Donny and the guys had some problems at the site and I -" Crystal senses that her husband is lying through his teeth. She quickly interrupts, "Forgot about the appointment, didn't you?" Playfully, the receptionist interjects, "Bad boy, Jack. Want me to spank him, Crystal?" Crystal takes Jack's hand and steps away towards the corridor. She tells her husband, "Com'on, Jack, we better go see Nancy before I lose you to Miss Hot Thang." Jack grins then utters, "But I like Miss Hot Thang." Crystal playfully elbows Jack's rib cage.

Towards the end of the long corridor, a few doors down from the intake rooms, Jack and Crystal are walking towards the OB/GYN section. Crystal eyes a pregnant lady with an envious stare as she passes by. Coming up the hallway cradling an armful of folders, is Ms. Thompson, the clinic's director. Crystal slyly steps behind Jack, trying to hide her bare feet as they near Ms. Thompson. "That's my boss," Crystal whispers to Jack. While passing Crystal and Jack, wearing a straight face, Ms. Thompson comments rhetorically, "Givin' away your shoes again, Crystal?" As Ms. Thompson disappears into her office along the corridor, Crystal leads Jack to a door marked, 'DR. NANCY KAMINSKI, GYNECOLOGIST.' Crystal softly knocks on the door. Behind the door, Nancy's voice answers, "It's open." Jack and Crystal enters. Attired in her white smock, Nancy sits at her desk dipping a peeled banana into a cup of strawberry yogurt.

The walls are covered with colorful, detailed posters of a woman's reproductive organs and the first, second and third stages of pregnancy. Nancy stirs the yogurt with the banana then takes a bite. Crystal and Jack takes a seat across from Nancy's desk. Crystal seems relaxed as if she's been in Nancy's office many times before. While eating, Nancy comments," Mmmm. This is sooo gooooood. Want some, guys?" Turning up their noses, Jack and Crystal quickly shake their heads 'no.' Nancy takes another small bite of her yogurt-dipped banana, wipes her mouth then tosses the left-overs into a nearby trash can. Nancy's face turns serious as she looks at Crystal and Jack, "Okay, down to business now." Crystal straightens her posture as she sits then looks at Nancy attentively. Jack sighs and still wishes that he was elsewhere. Anxiously anticipating Nancy's comments, Crystal crosses her fingers. Nancy turns to Crystal and begins to speak in a very professional tone, "Crystal, I looked at all of the lab tests, all of your exam charts, pap smear results, everything and you're absolutely fertile...without a doubt. I see no medical reason why you can't get pregnant." Nancy turns to Jack with a bit of concern and apprehension in her face. Crystal also turns to Jack with a bit of curiosity.

"Jack, after looking at-," the doctor is interrupted. Jack interjects, "Why's everybody looking at me like that for? What'd I do?" Wearing a no-nonsense expression, Nancy continues, "Jack, all lab tests and exam reports point to one conclusion...A low sperm count. Jack, had you ever had problems with this in the past?"

Nancy's question strikes a nerve in Jack. In protest of Nancy's query, Jack tightens his mouth and repositions himself in his chair. Crystal softly places her hand upon Jack's knee. Jack inches his knee away, rejecting his wife's loving support. Jack turns to the doctor with frustration in his eyes then utters, "I thought you was supposed to be our friend and was gonna help us." Jack turns to Crystal and releases more steam, "I knew we shouldn't had came here. We can afford a private doctor. I don't need to be-." Nancy interrupts, "Jack, listen to me. I am trying to help. Low sperm count isn't that uncommon. It's nothing to be ashamed of. Sometimes it's caused by something psychological." Jack's fed up. He stands to leave then spits out, "Now you calling me crazy, Nancy?" Shaking her head in disbelief at her husband's behavior, Crystal raises her voice a little, "Jack, sit down! You're being silly. Nancy's our friend. She's being honest and only trying to help." Jack has his hand on the door knob. The doctor quickly fires another bomb at him, "Jack, is there something you're keeping bottled up maybe?" Pissed, Jack opens the door to leave then says, "That's it. I'm leaving." Crystal sighs in disappointment then says, "Nancy, I'm sorry. He's just –." Nancy interjects by finishing Crystal's sentence, "Just a man. A big man who got his little male ego hurt, that's all. Crystal, take my advice. A vacation would do you both some good. Maybe this baby thing is a lit'l too much right now." Crystal replies, "You know, I've been trying to talk Jack into going to Virginia for my high school reunion but he keep making excuses about Donny and the guys needing him at the new site." Nancy shoots Crystal a look then schools her with, "Crystal, you need to let Jack know who's the real boss. Tell him that Donny and the guys can join him on the couch if he doesn't want to go to the reunion with you." Amused, Crystal cracks a smile as she stands to leave.

While stepping out into the hallway, Crystal says, "Thanks for all your help, Nancy." While gazing at Crystal's bare feet, Nancy says, "Hey, good luck with Mister Macho Man and by the way, um...you need a lit'l cash 'til pay day? Whatcha' need, a twenty? Thirty? Can thirty get you a good pair of sneakers?" Amused by Nancy's sense of humor, Crystal smiles as she continue down the corridor.

Later that night, two blocks from the beach at 1511 Oceanview Lane, the Canadays' two-story home luminates under the moonlit sky. Exotic palm trees line the street near their luxurious house nestled behind a paved, circled driveway. Jack's red Toyota Pathfinder is parked behind his wife's stylish black Jaquar with vanity plates reading, 'CRYSTAL.'

In an unfinished room resembling a baby nursery, scantly cladded in her tantalizing, see- through night gown, sad-eyed Crystal quietly fiddles with the brightly colored animals of a dangling mobile hovering above a toy-filled crib. From another part of the house, Jack's voice is heard,

"Crystal? Crystal? Where are you? You coming to bed?" Preoccupied with wishful thoughts, Crystal finger-brushes a stuffed teddy bear resting in the crib then slowly steps away towards the door.

In the master bedroom, under an elegant canopy bed, Jack is partially tucked underneath the covers. He's channel-surfing with the remote as the TV, perched atop a mirrored dresser, flickers different shades throughout the room. Minutes later, Crystal enters. The flickering TV light animates her curvaceous body through her sexy, translucent gown.

"I was calling you. 'Been hanging out in the nursery?," Jack asks. Crystal ignores Jack's question. Abruptly, Crystal turns on her Southern belle charm with a seductive smile and sensual bedroom eyes then coolly glides underneath the blankets next to Jack. Crystal begins to smother her husband with tender kisses all over his face and neck. The TV remote falls from Jack's fingertips as Crystal drowns him with soft, wet kisses upon his lips. While kissing and tenderly suckling his lips, Crystal softly asks, "Jack, do you love me?" Captivated by Crystal's charm, Jack responds, "You're the best thing that ever happened to me." While planting tender, juicy kisses upon Jack's lips, Crystal smoothly slides her right hand between Jack's legs then whispers, "Would you do anything for me?" Jack moans in pleasure as he feels Crystal's hand slowly massaging his inner-thighs then softly answers, "Anything." Crystal's hand slowly strokes Jack's rising penis as he moans louder in arousing pleasure. Crystal asks, "Can we go to my high school reunion in Virginia?" Caught up in the moment, Jack quickly answers, "Yes. Anything you want." Suddenly, Crystal freezes, leaving Jack completely baffled. Crystal slides out of the bed. Teasingly, Crystal stands at the edge of the bed with her arms folded and eying Jack as he aches for her return. Jack pleads, "Aw, com'on. You're so mean." Crystal replies, "So that's all it took for you to agree to go to my reunion?" Wearing a straight face, Jack bluntly answers, "Yep." The room abruptly darkens and falls silent as Jack kills the TV with a quick tap on the remote. Crystal slowly removes the sexy gown from her sensuous body, crawls back underneath the blankets then snuggles next to her waiting husband. Jack smiles triumphantly as he gently climbs on top of his inviting wife. "You guys are so easy," Crystal says. "Yep," Jack frankly replies.

CHAPTER TWO

The Reunion

A United 747 airliner lands on the runway at busy Duties International Airport in Washington, D.C. In the midst of a horde of travelers standing around the rotating conveyor, Jack and Crystal are retrieving their luggage off of the slow-moving belt. Moments later, at the National Car Rental service desk, Jack is accepting a set of keys from the sales clerk.

Traveling south on Interstate 95, Jack's behind the wheel glancing at the gas gauge. Crystal's staring out of the window, admiring the lofty, green Virginia pines flanking the busy freeway. Jack comments, "We're getting low on gas." Crystal replies, "I think there's a big truck stop coming up soon." Amazed by the scenery, Crystal continues, "God, I can't believe how green everything is here, It looks so beautiful and peaceful." Teasingly, Jack says, "Hm, that's what I thought when I first met you. Man, I tell ya', looks certainly can be deceiving." Playfully, Crystal shoots Jack an evil eye.

A road sign displays, 'SHALLOW CREEK 2 MILES.' A short distance ahead, an exit leading to a vast truck stop has a mammoth sign towering over tall pines and oaks advertising, 'SERVICE CITY TRUCK STOP.' Trailing two eighteen-wheelers, Jack exits the freeway and follows the tractor-trailers to the truck stop.

A pleasing smile surfaces on Crystal's face as she silently reminisces of her younger days. Excitedly, Crystal says, "We're almost there. God, I can't believe it's been fifteen years already." Teasingly, Jack asks, "Are you gonna get mushy now and start singing your alma mater?" Crystal playfully slaps Jack's right leg then says, "Oh, stop...You know, I don't even know our alma mater." Jack looks upward as if he's speaking to God, "Thank you." Crystal fires a quick jab to Jack's right leg. "Ouch," Jack screeches.

The Canadays' white Ford rental is pulling into the self-service island next to gas pump eight. Fishing out his wallet, Jack steps out of the car then walks toward the store. Crystal peers out of the window, observing the scenery and activity of the spacious truck stop. The mammoth lot is filled with countless rows of parked tractor-trailers on the right side. A teenage girl, wearing a revealing halter top and skin-tight, jean shorts, slithers from the passenger-side door of a parked eighteen-wheeler then climbs up and slides into the partially open door of another parked truck nearby. A family restaurant with an adjacent travelers' gift shop and two enormous motels border the left side. Highlighted with glossy red lipstick, a teenage boy walking with an extreme feminine stride, exits a motel room then vanishes across the lot between the rolls of parked eighteen-wheelers. Crystal is approached at the passenger-side window by a purple haired, teenage girl, "Hi, I'm tryin' to get enough money to get some'em to eat." Without hesitation, Crystal immediately digs into her purse, fishes out two crumbled five dollar bills and extends them to the smiling teen. Crystal asks, "Where's your parents?"

Ignoring Crystal's question, the purple-hair girl spots Jack exiting the store then dash away to meet him halfway. The lively girl quickly stuffs the two wrinkled bills into her jeans as Jack nears the car. The teen greets Jack with the same line she'd used on Crystal, "Hi, I'm tryin' to get enough money to get some'em to eat." Jack asks, "Where's your mom and dad?" Before the girl is given a chance to respond, Crystal pokes her head out of the window and warns, "Jack, I gave her ten bucks already!" The hustling teen looks at Crystal with an angry sneer then speedily turns away and steps toward the store. Jack gases up the Ford Escort. Moments later, the energetic panhandler exits the store grasping two packs of cigarettes in her hand. Crystal pokes her head out of the window again and shouts, "you said you wanted to get something to eat!" The care-free girl completely ignores Crystal while unraveling the plastic film from one of the cigarette packs. After pumping the gas, Jack slides back behind the wheel as Crystal looks disappointed in herself. Jack glances at his wife and comments, "So she suckered you. Forget about it, honey...Should we get a room now or do you still wanna visit your parents first?"

Crystal answers, "It's still early and I'm too anxious to sleep." Jack starts the engine then says, "Your parents it is. Just show me the way."

৵৹

On their way to visit Crystal's parents, the Canadays take Main Street through Shallow Creek's business district. In the midst of colorful storefront windows, a boarded-up teen drop-in center is cushioned between a laundromat and Middleton's Drugstore. The plywood enclosing the teen drop-in center is covered with large, spray-painted words, 'GO HOME', 'WET MATCHES', 'GET OUT OF OUR TOWN', ect. Continuing along Main Street towards the edge of town, the Canadays' Ford Escort slows down as it passes Shallow Creek High School's marquee billboard reading...

WELCOME BACK CLASS OF '85!

At the far-end of Main Street sits a used car lot and the tallest structure of this small rural town, the massive Shallow Creek Christian Fellowship Church topped with an eye-catching golden steeple. As the Canadays' white Ford slowly cruises by, a group of six ominous men standing in front of the church stare at the passing Ford with uninviting faces.

A short distance ahead, Main Street transforms into rural Route 208, a curvy blacktop flanked by lengthy pines and thick oaks. Turning off of Route 208, the Canadays' Ford rental pulls under the stylish archway of Shallow Creek's extravagant cemetery. The artistic blacken letters gracing the metal arch invitingly reads, 'WELCOME TO GREEN HILLS.' The Canadays' white sedan slowly eases its way along a narrow, graveled driveway dividing the well-manicured grounds ornamented with numerous rows of impressive tombstones of all shapes and sizes. The slow-moving Ford comes to a stop. Crystal and Jack steps out of the car. Crystal solemnly walks toward two marbled headstones several feet away. Crystal's solemn face suddenly turns puzzled as she observes the bountiful bouquets of flowers left at the foot of her parents' graves. Jack is close behind, quietly placing his hands upon Crystal's shoulders as she kneels before the two marbled headstones.

The headstone on the left is inscribed...

MRS. PEGGY R. FOSTER

August 4, 1945 - March 12, 1985

The headstone to Crystal's right reads...

MR. FRANK D. FOSTER

January 11, 1944 - March 12, 1985

Suddenly, Jack turns his head towards the roaring sound of a lawn mower motor. Moments later, the cemetery groundskeeper, perched on his John Deere riding mower, pulls up next to the Canadays' Ford Escort. The senior gentleman kills the mower's engine then slowly dismounts from the cushioned seat. With a huge country smile, the old man happily greets Jack and Crystal, "How y'all folks doin' t'day? Y'all kin to de' Fosters?" Crystal quickly answers, "Hi, I'm Crystal and this is my husband Jack. I'm their daughter." The old man ponders, rubs his chin then excitedly utters, "Oh yeah! Well shit in my pants !" Amused, Jack and Crystal crack a smile as the old-timer continues, "You went out to California just a lit'l while after de' wreck, that's right. Well, you did right. Sometimes it's best just to go away an' get it off yo' mind. Ain't no sense in worryin'. Hell, all that cryin' an' carryin' on just makes the grave deeper." Wearing a curious expression, Crystal asks, "Can I ask you something? Are you the one putting these flowers here?" With an admiring grin, the old man answers, "Naw, not me. A black fella by de' name of Jalan comes 'bout every few weeks or so an' lay 'em down there." Jack's face contorts in confusion as he quietly stands behind his kneeling wife. A look of surprise surfaces upon Crystal's face as soon as she heard the name Jalan. Crystal offers no explanation to Jack. She smiles pleasingly while running her fingers along the colorful flower pedals at the base of her parents' headstones. The groundskeeper asks, "So, y'all stayin' long?" Crystal answers, "No, we just come for my school reunion tomorrow night then we'll be going back to California." The old man speaks with years of wisdom in his simple country words, "School reunion, huh? I don't like 'em thangs. Nowadays it seems like all people do is talk 'bout one 'nother like dogs. Hell, seems like it's a crime nowadays to care 'bout somebody...Well, betta get back to work. Nice meetin' y'all." Jack and the old gentleman shake hands goodbye as Crystal stands and says, "Bye now. Take care of yourself." As the groundskeeper climbs back on his mower, Jack silently looks at Crystal as if he's awaiting some type of explanation about the black man who leaves the flowers at her parents' graves. Crystal plants a tender kiss upon Jack's chin while stepping towards the car. Crystal offers no explanation but softly says, "Thanks for coming, Jack." Jack conceals his bewilderment behind a forced smile then says, "You may not believe this but Jack Canaday loves his wife and if she wants to do something then I'm there a hundred percent." Playfully, Crystal begins to look in all directions then teases, "What'd you do with my husband? Where's he?"

The following night at the Shallow Creek High School gym, a top forty band is bellowing out dance hits from the summer of 1985 as the lively thirty-ish crowd out on the dance floor tries their best to regain the youthful spirit and moves they'd possessed fifteen years ago. Tuxedos, ties and classy gowns seem to be the attire of choice. The dimly lit gym is colorfully decorated with several large CLASS OF '85 banners and bunches of balloons dangling from the ceiling. Along the right side a series of dining tables are aligned. Each table is elegantly draped with a white tablecloth topped with a lit candle and a vintage bottle of champagne on ice. Some couples are taking a break from the dance floor to enjoy their meal and refreshments as a small catering staff attend to their needs. Bountiful tables of snacks and finger foods are lined along the left wall. The band fades out a crowd-pleaser as the lead singer smoothly dives into another '85 chart topper. No one leaves the jam-packed dance floor as hips and thighs sway and move with ease and agility to the rhythmic beat pulsating throughout the gym.

A handsome, ponytailed Black man, oddly dressed in a long trench coat, jeans and tennis shoes, is helping himself at the tables on the left. The lone man stuffs handfuls of bite-size hot links, popcorn shrimps, chicken wings, cookies and cheese sticks into his many coat pockets while slowly moving from one table to the next.

Jack and Crystal are in the midst of the festive dancing crowd. Looking uncomfortable dressed in a dap-
per tuxedo and tie, Jack is a bit stiff as he tries to stay in
sync with the sensuous moves of his hip-swinging wife.
Crystal is delightfully enjoying herself as she dances in her
sexy gown, revealing her enticing cleavage and shapely
curves.

The band gradually fades the song to take a brief break.
The crowd on the dance floor slowly disperses. A sophis-
ticated-looking Black lady, accompanied by her husband,
is approaching Crystal and Jack as they make their way
through the scattering crowd. Standing with her right
hand resting on her hip, the poised black lady is in Crystal's
path. Putting on a phony smile, she extends her left hand to
Crystal for a shake then says, "Crystal Foster? Hi, remember
me? Debra. Well, Debra Gordon now. This is my husband,
Eddie." Instantly, Crystal's face begins to twist in discomfort
as Debra's presence triggers bad memories from their high
school days. Reluctantly, Crystal shakes Debra's hand while
masking her distaste behind a cordial smile. Halfheartedly,
Crystal responds, "Hi, sure I remember you. You look
great. I'm Crystal Canaday now. This is my husband, Jack."
Behind a cynical grin, Debra's shifty eyes quickly scans Jack
from head to toe then turns to Crystal and says, "Maybe
you're not color blind after all." Jack is puzzled by Debra's
remark. Crystal's pretentious smile suddenly vanishes as her
face tightens in resentment. Avoiding confrontation, Crystal
steps away, pulling Jack by his forearm. Jack asks, "What'd
she mean by that?" Crystal ignores Jack's question as she
heads toward their dining table, now tugging Jack by his
hand. They reach their table. Immediately, Jack summons

a waitress to their table to replenish his plate. Looking a little exhausted, Crystal flops down in her chair. She uses the napkin wrapped around her utensils to wipe her forehead. Abruptly,

Crystal's eyes widen in surprise while looking across the now-cleared dance floor. Crystal's eyes zero in on the handsome, ponytailed black gentleman standing next to the last snack table along the left wall. The strangely dressed man is nibbling on a cookie while steadily stuffing his coat pockets with sweet goodies.

Crystal silently rise from the table then utters, "Jack, I'll be back." Jack nods 'okay' as he jams his hungry mouth with big pieces of a dinner roll. Crystal makes her way across the empty dance floor. The band's brief break is over. The lead singer takes the center microphone and bellows to the crowd) "I know you guys remember this one!" On perfect cue, the band explodes with another upbeat '85 hit! Once again, the dance floor quickly comes alive with gyrating hips and thighs! Jack's view of Crystal is blocked by the suddenly swollen crowd on the dance floor. Crystal reaches her destination. Silently, Crystal stands behind the black, ponytailed gentleman as he fills his trench coat pockets with bite-size chocolate bars. Both amused and puzzled as she eyes the man's jeans and tennis shoes, Crystal softly taps the man's shoulder. Crystal asks, "Jalan? Jalan Simms?" The peculiar dressed man turns around. His eyes widen in surprise as a pleasing smile begins to take shape on his brown face. There's an awkward moment of silence as Crystal and the ponytailed gentleman look into each other's eyes with facial expressions that speak of fond memories. The handsome man invitingly opens his arms as Crystal, without hesitation, steps into his warm embrace. Overwhelmed, Crystal melts as she rests her head upon the gentleman's chest.

Back at the dining table Jack is sitting alone murdering a sizeable T-bone steak. Crystal's old high school rival, Debra, sneakingly creeps up to Jack's table and says, "Excuse me, Jack. I don't mean to disturb your meal but I think you should see something." Debra gestures Jack to stand as she points across the dance floor to Crystal and the ponytailed gentleman entwined in a warm hug.

Jack stands then his mouth suddenly drops in shock at what his eyes are seeing. Debra is loving every second of this as she tells Jack, "You betta watch them two. You couldn't separate 'em back in the day." Unbeknownst to Debra, the very sight of Black guys leaves a sour taste in Jack's mouth. For the first time ever Jack is witnessing his wife in the arms of a Black man. Jack's face tightens in a sudden rage! The moment is too overwhelming for Jack. Abruptly, he scurry off to the restroom. Debra coolly walks away wearing a triumphant grin.

Enraged and breathing heavily, Jack storms into the vacant bathroom! He steps in front of the middle sink. Looking like a crazed psycho, Jack peers into the mirror. As Jack stares into his own eyes disturbing images of the four black bullies confronting and manhandling him in the muddle school bathroom surfaces. Jack has never let himself get this far out of control. He snatches a piece of paper towel from the dispenser then quickly wipes his redden, sweaty face. Still peering into the mirror and realizing that he can't let Crystal or anyone else see him this way, Jack tries to talk himself down, "Calm down, Jack. That was years ago. This is now. Take deep breaths, Jack. Just calm down. Be mature about this, Jack. Just go back out there and handle this like a man, Jack. That's it's. Just go out there and -" Furious, Jack slams his fist atop the sink then spits out, "Damn! How can she do that to me?!" Abruptly, the door swings open. A concerned man strolls in and asks, "Is everything okay, fella?" Jack freezes, ignores the curious gentleman then awkwardly steps away from the sink and leaves.

Back out to the gym, along the left wall near the snack tables, Crystal and Jalan Simms, her Black boyfriend from the past, are standing romantically close as soft music lingers in the air. Looking at Jalan's strange attire with puzzled eyes, Crystal asks, "Jalan, um..is there a problem? Why are you dressed this way?" Jalan is edgy and seems anxious to leave. Jalan swipes a napkin from the refreshment table then asks, "Gotta pen?" Crystal shakes her head 'no' then hastily snatch a protruding pen from a passing waiter's pocket as he replenishes the bowls and plates of bite-size treats atop the tables. Jalan takes the pen from Crystal and quickly jots down his address on the napkin then hurriedly hands it to Crystal. Jalan sticks the pen back into the waiter's pocket as he turns to Crystal and says, "I can't explain it right now. Come by tonight, if you can." Baffled, Crystal scans the wrinkled napkin as Jalan hurriedly dash away, leaving the gym out of an unmarked side door. Jack approaches Crystal as she stands in a daze holding the crumbled napkin. Calmly, Jack says, "You don't owe me an explanation. We're both adults here-" Crystal rudely interrupt Jack and says, "Jack, we gotta go. We gotta go now. I think an ol' friend's in trouble. Something's just not right." Jack quickly replies, "Wait a minute, Crystal Yes, I agreed to come to this reunion, but now we gotta go play Batman and Robin?"

Crystal lowers her head to hide the watery eyes of her pleading face. Innocently, Crystal toys with the wrinkled napkin. Slowly, Crystal reels Jack in...Jack gives in.

Jack sighs then says, "Aw, com'on. I can't stand it when you get like this. So what's the story?" Relieved, Crystal rewards Jack with a tender 'thank you' kiss on his cheek. "I'm not sure yet, but we'll find out once we get to this address on this napkin," Crystal replies. Jack and Crystal leaves the reunion party through the front exit door. Across the dance floor, nosy Debra is looking at the exit door closing behind Crystal and Jack with a disappointing frown.

CHAPTER THREE

Jalan And The Teens

A short time later, along Route 208, the Canadays' white Ford Escort travels through Shallow Creek's heavily-wooded back country with its high beam lights on. The rental sedan turns off of the curvy blacktop onto a bumpy, dirt road shouldered by thick forest underbrush. Suddenly, the high beaming lights of the Canadays' rental illuminates a rundown, two-story house nestled on a partially cleared lot of leafy dogwoods, tall pines and thick oaks. The Canadays' white Ford comes to a stop. No other cars are parked outside. The front of the house quickly darkens as Jack shuts off the Escort's headlights. Jack and Crystal step out of the car then walks up to the leaning, weathered porch. The moonlit sky is throwing eerie tree shadows across the front yard. One of the two front windows is boarded up with thick plywood. Crystal is staying securely close to Jack's side as they softly walk up the creaky steps and leaning porch. Wearing a curious face, Jack turns to Crystal and utters, "Maybe we're at the wrong address. You sure we got the right address?" Crystal quickly answers, "That's what he wrote on the napkin." They reach the front door. Jack knocks on the door as Crystal stands poised to greet Jalan. Crystal and Jack look at one another with puzzled faces as they listen to a series of door latches being undone. The door opens. A brown-skinned, fifteen year old Latino girl covered with gang-styled tattoos and silver rings on her nostrils, left eyebrow and lower lip, appears in the doorway eating a cheese stick. This is Josie. In a very pleasant and friendly tone, Crystal says, "Hi. Is Jalan Simms here?" Josie eyes Jack's fancy tux and Crystal's elegant gown with a stiff upper lip then, with a slight Spanish accent, asks, "Who the fuck is you?" Josie's harsh words cause Crystal to step back as Jack comes forward. Jack tries to explain, "Listen, my wife's friend wrote this address down and told her to come by tonight." Josie rapidly fires back, "If that's true then why the fuck YOU here?" Jack sighs in relief as a sixteen year old, street-tough Black boy appears at the doorway next to Josie. This is Micky. Micky's nibbling on a large chocolate chip cookie. Micky turns to Josie and says, "Remember bitch, Jalan told us to look out for his ol' schoo buddy." Micky turns to Crystal then asks. "Ain't you Crystal?"

A sense of relief spreads across Crystal's face as she's happy to be speaking to anyone other than barking Josie. Crystal politely replies, "Yes, and this is my husband Jack."

Rudely, loud-mouth Josie inches forward in front of Micky and interjects, "Jalan ain't here right now. He went to look for Shelly. She's probably turnin' tricks again at Service City. He told that bitch to stop that shit but she don't listen though. Stupid ho." Stunned by Josie's speech, Crystal's face freezes as Jack shakes his head in disbelief. Micky tries to scold Josie, "Damn girl, you ain't gotta be broardcastin' everybody's business n' shit." Micky turns to Crystal and Jack and politely asks, "Y'all wanna come in n' chill for a minute?" Micky and Josie step aside as Jack and Crystal enters the house.

Micky shuts the door and meticulously locks all five door latches as Jack and Crystal step further into the living room. The long trench coat that Jalan had worn earlier at the school reunion party catches Crystal's eye as it hangs on a hook behind the front door.

The various snacks and finger foods Jalan had taken from the reunion party earlier this evening are laid out on a dog-chewed, corner-chipped coffee table in front of an old, scratched-up

Magnavox TV. The room is meagerly decorated with aging, yard sale-reject furniture and meaningless, dull pictures from a bygone era. Crystal and Jack are looking at Josie and Micky, awaiting an invitation to sit down on one of the two ripped, mismatched couches. Inconspicuously, Micky shifts his eyes to examine Crystal's curvaceous backside then says, "Mm girl, you got some nice swings in yo' backyard." Crystal blushes in response to Micky's remark then she turns to Jack and whispers, "See honey, I still got it." Jack leans back, peeps at Crystal's butt and replies, "That maybe true but instead of calling them swings I think they're more like a whole playground." Teasingly, Crystal shoots Jack a scornful eye. Amused at the couple's playful nature, Micky cracks a smile. Crystal is anxious to sit. She coughs, pretending to clear her throat. Josie nor Micky picks up on the hint. Concealing her sigh, Crystal asks, "Mind if we sit down?" Rudely, Josie dash and flops down on the couch directly in front of the heavily-nicked Magnavox. The snow-flaked, poor reception on the beat-up Magnavox causes Josie to groan, "Fuck! Crabby ass TV!" Micky gestures Crystal and Jack to take a seat on the other couch. Jack and Crystal sits down, both sink deeper than expected into the worn-out sofa. Micky gives Josie a look then turns to the Canadays and says, "Y'all gotta 'cuse Josie. The girl's not house-trained yet." Micky points to the plentiful snacks atop the table and politely utters, "Help yo'self." Crudely, Josie quickly reaches and grabs a handful of bite-size chocolate bars before Jack and Crystal gets a chance to. Wearing expressions of disbelief at Josie's behavior, Jack and Crystal exchange glances at one another.

Crystal turns to Micky and asks, "I'm sorry, what's your name?" In a wishful manner, as if Crystal was flirting with him, Micky grins from cheek to cheek then answers, "Micky." Crystal asks, "Micky, is it possible to get something to drink? My mouth's a little dry." Immediately, Micky turns his head towards the kitchen and yells, "YO ROBBIE! COLE! We got company! Got some lemonade or some'em in there? TWO SHOTS!" Jack and Crystal rubs Micky's echo out of their ears while glancing at one another.

Meanwhile, evil lurks outside as two beefy Dodge Ram pickups slowly pull onto the lot, parking next to the Canadays' rental. The six ominous-looking men who were standing in front of the church earlier are now sitting quietly in the parked trucks, eying the shabby two-story house with strong displeasure.

Back inside, a squeaky door opens on the left side of the living room. A skinny, light-skinned seventeen year old Black boy enters the front room carrying two glasses of orange- flavored Kool-aid. Micky looks at the Canadays and says in a cynical tone, "That's Cole. He's our house nigga." There's a little tension between Cole and Micky. Cole totally ignores Micky...He never made eye contact with Micky as he entered the room. Close behind Cole is an over-weight, sixteen year old White boy with an acoustic guitar strapped across his right shoulder. This is Robbie. Cole politely offers the tall glasses of Kool-aid to Crystal and Jack as Robbie begins to slowly strum his guitar strings, gradually building up to a little ditty with a strong country rhythm. Josie turns up her upper lip then tells Robbie, "Man, nobody wanna hear that hillbilly shit!"

Rudely, Josie stretches across the snack-covered coffee table to turn up the TV volume. Then, abruptly...BOOM! CRACK! Two empty beer bottles burst through the side window! The window shatters! Glass pieces crumble to the floor! The teens seem uncannily calm...somewhat prepared for this routine. Micky yells, "Get down!" Cole quickly hits the light switch as everyone drops to the floor. The room darkens with a cold silence then Crystal asks, "What's going on? Where's Jalan?"

In the vast parking lot of the Service City Truck Stop, ponytailed Jalan is hastily running in between parked rows of eighteen-wheelers in search of the missing girl from his makeshift teen shelter. Jalan calls out, "Shelly? Shelly?" Suddenly, a purple-hair girl in unbuttoned skin-tight shorts crawls out of a trucker's cab door. Her left breast is spilling out of her crooked halter top. This is the same care-free girl who'd swindled Crystal out of ten dollars to buy cigarettes at the gas station the day before. As Shelly's feet reach the ground, she begins to clinch her stomach. Her face twists in pain. She doubles over as oozing vomit spills out of her mouth. Jalan spots Shelly as she throws up again. Jalan's face flattens in disappointment as if he's seen this scene once too many times. Silently, Jalan sighs as he straightens Shelly's crooked halter top then pushes her left breast back into place. Again, Jalan sighs as he reach around Shelly's waist to button her shorts. Placing his arms underneath her arm pits, Jalan helps Shelly to stand up straight as her weakly legs begin to buckle. "Com'on Shelly. Let's go home," Jalan says. Meanwhile, things have intensified in the front yard of Jalan's shelter in the deep woods of Shallow Creek. Standing firm ten feet from the front porch, Jack is brandishing a mop handle as Crystal waves a broom handle at the six angry men. Poised and ready to strike, Jack and Crystal keep the fierce-looking six at bay. One of the ominous men steps forward, just mere inches away from Jack's mop handle. Jack quickly jabs the lengthy handle at the man's growling face. The grimly man steps back from Jack's flourishing weapon. Micky, Josie, Cole and Robbie are standing on the creaky porch. Josie and Micky looks anxious to rumble as Cole and Robbie calmly observe Jack and Crystal hold their ground. Not one to hold her tongue, Josie yells, "Won't y'all redneck motherfuckers leave us the fuck alone!" In an uneducated, thick Southern drawl, one of the infuriated men lets off steam, "Why don't cha all just do us a favor an' just go back to wherever the hell ya' came from." Another ominous man interjects, "Y'all ain't gonna come here and contaminate MY HOMETOWN! Y'all SICK an' ain't nobody gonna want y'all! Y'all ain't good for NOTHIN'! A bunch of wet matches! Useless!"

Enraged, Micky charges down the porch steps! Crystal frantically yells, "Micky, get back! Micky! Get back!" Reluctantly, Micky freezes but spits out, "Fuck 'em rednecks! They don't scare me!"

Another raunchy man steps forward. He stares at Micky and snarls, "Boy, you betta listen to the lit'l lady fo' ya' get ya'self hurt now." Tight-fisted and fired up, Micky charges forward as Jack and Crystal step closer to block his path. Jack utters, "Don't Micky." Suddenly, bouncing headlights flicker between the towering pines and oaks, stealing everyone's attention. A rusty, '86 Jeep Cherokee speedily enters the lot. Dipping into every pothole, the rugged Jeep bounces and swerves around the two hardy Dodge Ram pickups and the Canadays' rental then comes to a stop a few feet from the front porch. Sitting behind the wheel of the Jeep Cherokee, Jalan gestures to Shelly to lay down. Shelly's head quickly disappears. Heated, Jalan jumps out from the driver-side door brandishing a .22 gauge rifle at the six rugged men! "Get off of our property!," Jalan yells. The wrathful six isn't moving a muscle. The mean-looking bunch makes quick, inconspicuous glances at one another but never budged an inch.

POW! POW! Jalan fires two shots into the air! The resounding gunshots echo throughout the woods. Crystal is completely stunned as she gazes at Jalan holding the rifle. Jalan shouts at the men, "Leave!" Reluctantly, the six scraggy men slowly back away then climb into their hefty trucks. Each of the men shoots an evil gaze at Jalan. Both sides know that this fight isn't over yet. The two Dodge Rams hurriedly spin away out of the front yard. Jalan hides his rifle back into his beat-up Cherokee. He stuffs it underneath the front seat. Groaning in pain, Shelly stumbles out of the Cherokee's passenger-side door. Once again, Crystal is totally blown away with surprise as she recognizes Shelly's purple hair. Crystal drops her broom then hurriedly rush to assist Shelly. Crystal tucks her right arm underneath Shelly's left arm pit and asks, "Remember me? I gave you ten dollars at the gas station—" Rudely, Shelly interjects, "And?" Disappointed in Shelly's cold response, Crystal sighs while kindly helping the weak- legged teen in taking baby steps toward the porch.

The excitement is over. Josie, Robbie, Micky and Cole goes back inside the house. Jalan politely step towards Jack with his hand extended for a friendly shake. Jack is still holding the long-handle mop. Jalan says, "Hey thanks for lookin' out for us. And nice weapon you got there...I'm Jalan." Jack places the mop aside to shake Jalan's hand then says, "Some friendly neighbors you got around here, huh? Hi, I'm Jack Canaday. Crystal's husband." Abruptly, Jalan freezes with a peculiar, somewhat amused grin then glances back at Crystal as she helps Shelly up the porch steps. "Jack, you're a lucky man," Jalan says. Jokingly, Jack responds, "Well, maybe n—" Overhearing the guys' every word, Crystal quickly interjects, "Jack!" Admiring the couple's sense of humor, Jalan smiles. Jack turns to Jalan with a touch of seriousness, "Thanks...

She's a keeper. By the way, your friendly neighbors took out one of your windows." In a very cynical tone, Jalan replies, "Love thy neighbor. Break thy neighbor's windows. Don'tcha just love this country, Jack?" Jack picks up the broom and mop from the ground as he and Jalan exchange small talk while shuffling behind Crystal and Shelly slowly making it to the front door.

 ❧

A few hours later, Jalan's makeshift shelter is calm and peaceful. Jack is stretched out asleep on one of the torn sofas. He's comfortably nestled in the bosom of his loving wife. Crystal is wide awake. Uninterested in the late-night program, she mindlessly gazes at the bad reception on the screen of the old Magnavox. Something else is weighing more heavily on her mind. Crystal turns her head towards the closed kitchen door as she hear chatter from Jalan and the teens.

Behind the closed door, Jalan is standing at the kitchen table stirring five tall glasses filled with a foamy, dark-colored concoction. Nearby, a partially open cabinet reveals an entire shelf of prescription bottles. A small, unlocked padlock dangles from the latch of the open cabinet. Sitting at the kitchen table, Josie and Micky are having some fun teasing Jalan while awaiting their drinks. Josie asks, "So Jalan, I betcha back in the day you was a player, huh? Did Crystal give up the booty?" Amused by Josie's humor, Jalan cracks a smile. Robbie is softly plucking the strings of his guitar...tuning it perhaps. Shelly's head is resting upon her arms atop the table. She looks exhausted. Cole is quietly scribbling something into his pocket-size writing pad. Micky eyes Jalan while wearing an admiring grin then says, "My man's cool. He probably got all 'em girls wit' that pony-tail. He probably dropped a line like 'I let you touch my hair if you let me touch yo' yang-yang...Black, White, red, yellow. I betcha my man had 'em all." The kitchen is filled with giggles and laughter for a brief moment. And then, the light-hearted chuckles suddenly cease as clean-cut, straight-faced Cole interjects his thoughts, "Jalan didn't even have a ponytail in high school. And he and Crystal probably had a tight plutonic relationship. You know, the kind -" Micky rudely interrupts, "Cole, man, just shut the hell up!" Backing up Micky, Josie turns to Cole and says, "You sho' know how to kill a party, don'tcha?" Chubby Robbie cools the heated moment with a playful country ditty as he softly strums his guitar. Robbie sings, "Jalan had a white girl back in nineteen eighty-five...It amazes me that the brother is walkin' around an' still alive."

The playful camaraderie between Jalan and the free-spirited teens is a routine ritual in the kitchen. Jalan grins amusingly at Robbie's teasing song. He is through stirring the five foamy drinks. Carefully, Jalan places a glass in front of each teen. Robbie leans his six-string up against the leg of the kitchen table. Jalan softly taps Shelly upon her head, acknowledging that her drink is ready. Obediently, each of the colorful teens quietly swallow the dark, foamy liquid, finishing it to the last drop...each realizing that this awful-tasting stuff is their lifesaver. Nodding with a satisfied expression, Jalan says, "Alright guys, say goodnight to our guests then go to bed." The teens scatter out of the kitchen. Jalan locks the cabinet then takes the empty glasses from the table. He quickly rinses them out then places them in the sink.

❧

A few minutes later in the living room, the snow-flaked TV screen is illuminating Crystal's pretty face as she nestles Jack upon her warm bosom. Jalan quietly walks into the room. Crystal is unaware of Jalan's presence. With a touch of envy in his eyes, Jalan silently gaze at Crystal being a human pillow for her sleeping husband.

Jalan whispers, "Crystal. Crystal. Wanna talk?" Crystal lifts her head to look at Jalan. He gestures her to join him outside on the porch.

Extremely slowly and very carefully, Crystal inches her way from underneath her heavy, sleeping husband. Jalan creeps toward the front door and begins to quietly undo the five latches.

The moonlit sky adds to the romantic ambience of the night as Jalan and Crystal sit comfortably close on the steps of the leaning, weathered porch. They reminisce about the old days and catch up on the new.

"To see you holding that gun tonight had to be the most shocking thing I'd ever seen," Crystal says.

Jalan grins then replies, "Times have changed, Crystal. I've changed. Adjusted is probably a better word...It was tough when you left. How come you stopped writing?" "Jalan, if it wasn't for your friendship after my parents died I probably would've went crazy. You was really there for me and I'll never forget that. But...I don't know. After awhile I just needed a change of scenery and when I got accepted at

UCLA I guess I used that as the perfect excuse to get away," Crystal sighs then affectionately runs her fingers along Jalan's ponytail. There's a moment of silence as the two high school sweethearts briefly gaze into each other's eyes then Crystal continues, "Your letters became harder to read and you became a fantasy, knowing that we were too far apart to keep anything going...And then I met Jack. I'm sorry, Jalan. I never meant to hurt you."

Jalan responds, "Yes, I know. Jack seems like a nice guy. I'm happy for you, Crystal. Met at UCLA?" Crystal nods, "He was an architect-engineering major...Now he got his hands in real estate and contracting." A pleasing thought crosses Jalan's mind. He places his hand upon Crystal's knee while grinning cheek to cheek. Jalan asks, "Remember when we promised to help at least ten thousand people before we died?"

Crystal replies, "You know, I think I'm getting close to my quota. I work at a health clinic. And you, well -"

Jalan interjects, "Well, I think I still gotta ways to go yet." Crystal's face turns extremely serious as she asks, "Jalan, what's the story on the kids? Runaways?" "Society's throwaways is more exact. Truckers bring 'em in from all over. And the only way they knew how to survive was to sell themselves," Jalan answers.

"And that's where you come in. You're all they have, huh?" Crystal asks while wearing an admiring grin.

Somewhat modestly Jalan utters, "Pretty much." Crystal leans closer and rewards Jalan with a tender kiss on his cheek. In complete silence, both Jalan and Crystal peer up at the moonlit sky. They seem to be both reminiscing about their times together fifteen years ago. Crystal breaks the silence and says, "You're a great man Jalan Simms...And hey, thanks for putting the flowers on my parents' graves. The old man at the cemetery told us. Must be costing you a fortune." "No, not at all. I get the free day-olds and um..some other things I need from the drugstore in town," Jalan replies. He ponders a moment then flashes a huge reminiscing grin across his face. As Jalan's mind hark back to high school years, he utters, "Remember when you introduced me to your father for the very first time? I was so scared and nervous about the color thing. And Frank went to shake my hand and told me to go to the bathroom and wash the dirt off my face then he just busted out laughing so hard when I started rubbin' my face, thinkin' I actually had dirt on my face...Frank was such a cool dude. And yo' mother - the best chocolate chip cookies in town!" Crystal smiles amusingly, then somewhat flirtatiously, brushes her shoulder against Jalan's. Suddenly, the front door rapidly squeaks open. Jack storms out onto the porch! Towering over Jalan and Crystal, tight-faced Jack wants an explanation. He looks dead into Crystal's eyes and barks, "What's this, Crystal? You didn't even have the decency to introduce us and now this!" Crystal sighs then shakes her head in disbelief at Jack's behavior. Jack turns to Jalan then continues his barking, "You wanna screw her?" Jack's nose is inches from Jalan's face. Crystal quickly rises. Defiantly, Crystal stands between Jack and Jalan. Pissed at her barking husband, Crystal shouts, "That's it, Jack! We're leavin'! Let's go now, Jack. Jalan didn't deserve that. Let's go, Jack!" Guilt slowly sips into Jack's face. Crystal steps away. She heads toward their Ford Escort parked several feet from the porch. Standing close to Jalan, Jack looks embarrassed. Jack wants to apologize but can't seem to find the right words, "Hey, I don't -" Smoothly, Jalan interjects, "Don't sweat it, Jack. I understand." Jalan glances at Crystal then quickly turns back to Jack and utters, "You better go patch things up before you become single like me." Crystal looks totally pissed as her hand grasps the Escort's driver-side door handle.

Crystal looks back and says, "Jalan, I'll come by tomorrow to say goodbye before we leave town." She eyes her husband with an angry frown then utters, "Com'on Jack!" Jack shuffles to the Escort's passenger-side door. He avoids eye contact with Crystal as her piercing stare scorns his every move.

The Canadays have checked themselves into the motel near the Service City Truck Stop. Jack is asleep, buried beneath the covers of their comfortable bed. Crystal can't sleep. She seems preoccupied with other matters as she paces the floor. Periodically, she glances out of the window observing the night activity of the massive truck stop. The flickering neon lights illuminate Crystal's sheer night gown and her tantalizing body as she gazes out the window.

Crystal leaves the window then walks next to the bed. She stands over her sleeping husband. Something is weighing heavily on her mind. She stares at Jack as if she wants to wake him but suddenly steps away. Crystal begins to pace the floor again.

At the truck stop gas station a husky pickup is parked at pump four. It's the beefy Dodge Ram that one of the six ominous-looking men was driving earlier at Jalan's teen shelter. The rugged redneck who'd gotten Micky heated is filling up a two-gallon gas can. Two of the other rough-looking rednecks are inside the store. Each of the three men seem anxious...up to something mischievous, perhaps.

Back in the motel room, Crystal gazes out of the window at the truck stop night activity. Her enticing curves are outlined through her translucent night gown. It's the wee hours of the night. The gas station is vacant. The rednecks' Dodge Ram pickup is gone. In the midst of the vast parking lot where lengthy eighteen-wheelers are aligned, Crystal's eyes zero in on a girlish, teenage boy sliding out of a trucker's cab door.

Crystal doesn't like what she sees. She closes the window curtain then begins to pace and glance at her sleeping husband as if she wants to wake him. Crystal seems very edgy...preoccupied with a hundred thoughts racing across her mind. Finally, Crystal walks over to the bed. She lightly shoves Jack's shoulder, "Jack. Jack. Wake up. We gotta go back, Jack. We gotta go back!"

Jack rubs the sleep out of his eyes then looks at his wife's desperate, pleading eyes. Jack sighs, "Batman and Robin again?"

"Jack, I'm worried about the kids. We gotta go back," Crystal replies.

"Now?" Jack asks.

"Please, Jack?" Crystal pleads.

Jack sighs while crawling out of bed. Jack and Crystal migrate to the tiny closet where a few of their belongings are hung. Jack searches for a pair of pants. Crystal hastily finds a quick slip-over dress and is ready to go.

Teasingly, Jack says, "You know, I'm thinking about divorcing you." Crystal's not in the mood for Jack's playfulness right now. She quickly replies, "That's fine. Let's just go and check on the kids first."

A short time later, in the deep woods of Shallow Creek, high-beam lights flicker through the forest trees along Route 208. The Canadays' Ford Escort turns off of the curvy blacktop and is suddenly bumper-to-bumper...head-on with the ominous rednecks' beefy Dodge Ram pickup coming out of the bumpy, dirt road which leads to Jalan's makeshift teen shelter. The front bumpers of the Canadays' rental and the Dodge Ram are only mere inches apart as the beaming headlights illuminate the three laughing, sinister faces in the meaty pickup. Jack repeatedly pounds his palm on the horn! Honk! Honk! Honk!

The big Ram isn't budging an inch.

Abruptly, Crystal's eyes widen in surprise as she sees bellowing smoke rise high into the moonlit sky a short distance away above the tree tops near Jalan's teen shelter. Frantically, Crystal turns to Jack while pointing at the rising clouds of smoke, "Go around them, Jack! The house's on fire! Look!" Rapidly, Jack shifts into reverse, floors the gas, speedily spins and fishtails it around the steadfast Ram!

One of the sinister-looking men pokes his head out of the Ram's window and laughingly yells, "Y'all folks have a goodnight now!" The Canadays' rental quickly vanishes down the bumpy, dirt road leading to Jalan's makeshift shelter. The weathered, two-story shack is engulfed with orange flames and smoke shooting out of the second floor windows as growing blazes climb along the right exterior wall.

Several yards from the porch near Jalan's Jeep Cherokee, half asleep and dressed in their night clothes, Shelly, Josie and Micky are standing close together awaiting the others to exit the enflamed house. The rapidly growing flames are spreading wildly over the entire structure!

Draped in kiddie-colored pajamas and surprisingly calm, Cole exits the front door juggling an armful of clothes on the left and a handful of CD'S, his writing pad and a skinny Sony walkman dangling on his right. Cole drops his clothes next to Shelly then aims his butt and flops down atop the tiny pile of jeans, t-shirts, ect. Somewhat nonchalantly, Cole inserts a REM CD into his walkman and positions the headphones while gazing at the flourishing flames covering the house. Cole is an avid REM fan and most of his CD's are from alternative rock bands.

Standing nearby, Micky and Josie glance at the white faces on the covers of Cole's CD's then grimace in disbelief. Micky can't restrain his thoughts as he turns to Josie and utters, "That's why the high-yella' motherfucker's so confused now. He be listenin' to the wrong music. Brother think he be white an' shit." Micky and Josie share a lighthearted chuckle at Cole's expense. Their reaction is nothing new to Cole. It seems like Cole's been either misunderstood or given the third degree treatment ever since he was a little boy growing up on the mean side of North Philly.

Things really hit the fan when Cole was fourteen and his crackhead mother kicked him out after learning of his published letter-to-the-editor newspaper article complaining about the abundance of crack dealers in his neighborhood.

Inside the burning house, dense smoke and fierce flames are beginning to crawl along the kitchen ceiling. Jalan is hastily grabbing various medicine bottles from the unlatched cabinet and hurriedly stuffing the prescription bottles into a draw-string laundry bag. Jalan dash out of the kitchen as the invading flames creep towards the cabinets!

Just as he'd left it earlier, Robbie's guitar is still leaning up against the leg of the kitchen table.

Meanwhile, back outside, chubby Robbie slowly jogs out the front door with an armful of clothes. Big Robbie joins the teens already mustered outside near Jalan's rusty Cherokee. Totally unaware, Robbie's pajama bottoms have slipped, exposing a sizeable portion of his pale buttocks. Josie looks at Robbie with a peculiar expression then asks, "Where's yo' guitar?" A look of total astonishment suddenly covers Robbie's face then smoothes out to a pleasing smile. Puzzled by Robbie's expression, Josie asks, "Why ya' lookin' at me like that?"

Still grinning, Robbie replies, "You do care 'bout me, huh?"

Josie quickly interjects, "Motherfucker, shut yo' white fat ass up an' just tell me where yo guitar's at!"

Micky can no longer conceal his secret desire for Josie.

Micky glances at Josie with opportune eyes. This is his one-shot chance to impress her...to be

her hero. Abruptly, Micky dash away towards the burning shack and yells, "I know where his guitar's at!"

Josie peeps at Robbie's pale buttocks and utters, "Man, pull 'em pajamas up!"

Jalan exits the front door with the weighty, stuffed laundry bag as Micky quickly passes by.

Jalan turns his head and warns, "Be careful, Mick! You only got about two minutes before she goes!"

"I will," Micky confidently replies.

The Canadays' Ford Escort rapidly swerves and enters the front yard. Micky burst through the front door with Robbie's guitar in his right hand as the entire flaming second floor caves in!

Sparks and burning pieces of wood spit out upon the lawn!

Standing next to their most prized possessions, Jalan and the teens helplessly stand safely near the Jeep watching the menacing, unforgiving flames flatten the entire house into a pile of glowing hot ash!

Jack and Crystal are awestruck as they observe the burning destruction from their car. As the dancing flames throw flickering shadows on their faces, Crystal turns to Jack with a determined look in her eyes and says, "Jack, one of the new houses –" Jack interjects, "Not even finished yet, Crystal."

With that sure-fire look of hers, Crystal quickly says, "They can stay with us until one of them is finished. We'll figure out the finances later. I'll pay for it myself if I have to."

"You got it all figured out, don'tcha Crystal? How long you've been thinking about this?" Jack asks.

"Since we first met them," Crystal solemnly replies.

"So now you're Mother Teresa?" Jack remarks.

Pleadingly, Crystal explains, "Jack, we gotta chance to make a difference in their lives. They need us. How can we go back to that big empty house knowing that these kids got no place to call home?"

Jack sighs then slowly cracks a smile. He quips, "Okay, but I'm divorcing you as soon as I get a chance."

Pleased, Crystal puckers her lips and rewards Jack with a big juicy smack on his surprised lips.

The morning sun breaks, slowly illuminating the dusky sky over Shallow Creek. At the edge of town, on the far-end of Main Street, Honest Harry is unlocking the office trailer on his used car lot. The roadside lot consists of two rows of late-model sedans, wagons, pickups and vans ornamented with colorful balloons tied to antennas and door handles.

A large sign atop the office trailer proudly boasts...

HONEST HARRY'S USED CARS
HONEST PRICES ! - HONEST ANSWERS!

Honest Harry steps inside the small office trailer. Jalan's rusty '86 Jeep Cherokee enters the tot. The Canadays' rental is following close behind Jalan's Jeep. Both vehicles are packed with stuffed bags and tiresome, sleepy-eyed teens. Jalan and Jack park their cars in front of the office trailer. Honest Harry steps out to greet his first customers of the morning. Only Jack and Jalan gets out. Crystal and the teens stay put inside the Cherokee and Escort. Honest Harry is wearing a big ol' country smile as he approaches Jalan and Jack.

Honest Harry and Jalan seems to know each other. Harry greets, "Mornin', Jalan. How's that piece of shit rust bucket runnin'?"

Amused by Harry's colorful language, both Jack and Jalan crack a smile as Jalan replies, "Not bad. Not bad, Harry."

Donning a sincere straight face, Harry rapidly fires back, "You're a damn liar, Jalan. That Jeep was a piece of shit when I sold it to ya' and it's still a piece of shit. Didn't I tell ya' not to buy it?

But nah, you wanted it anyway...What can I do for y'all this mornin'?"

Jalan politely introduces Jack, "Harry, this is my friend Jack." Jack and Honest Harry shake hands as Jalan continues, "We're taking the kids to California. You got anything that could hold eight people?"

"Sho' do. Right over yonder here," Honest Harry replies while leading Jalan and Jack towards an extended, white Carrier van parked at the left end of the back row.

"California, huh? Well, I wouldn't trust drivin' this thing that far, but this' all I got to carry that

kinda' load," Honest Harry says.

The three men walk closer to the rust-spotted '79 Chevy Carrier van and observe the fading, thin layer of white paint covering bold, black letters on both sides reading...

SHALLOW CREEK CHRISTIAN FELLOWSHIP CHURCH

Jalan wonders what Jack thinks of the old church van. Jalan looks at Jack. In response, Jack nods 'okay.'

Jack knows a thing or two about mechanics. He turns to Harry and asks, "Any major problems with the transmission or the engine?"

"Like I told ya', I wouldn't drive it ten miles outta town...but it run though. Hell, it might breakdown 'fo ya' cross the state line, or if ya' say yo' prayers right ya' could make it all the way to California. Y'all want it?" Harry replies.

Jack asks, "What 'you asking for it?"

"Thirteen hundred," Harry replies.

Jalan interjects, "Minus the trade-in of my Cherokee and my twenty-two."

Honest Harry glances at Jajan's rusty Cherokee then turns up his upper lip in disgust. Harry ponders a moment. He scratches his head then utters, "Eleven hundred-fifty. Hundred forty for the rust bucket. Ten for yo' rifle."

"Aw, com'on Harry. A hundred an' fifty bucks? That's all?" Jalan protests.

"Eleven-fifty," Harry firmly utters. Jalan looks extremely concerned about Harry's asking price.

Confidently, Jack fishes out his wallet, quickly pulls out his GOLD CREDIT CARD and coolly hands it to Harry. Happily, Honest Harry accepts Jack's shiny card.

Jacks proudly says, "Not a problem. We'll take it. Can you make sure the Escort gets back to

National Rental for me?"

"Sonny, if yo' card's any good I'll take that son-of-a-bitch back my own damn self," Harry quips then steps away toward the office trailer.

Harry continues, "Y'all com'on in. Let's see if this card got some real gold in it."

Jack and Jalan follow Harry towards the trailer steps. Jack briefly looks back at Crystal sitting in the Escort. Jack points to the old church van and gestures Crystal to get the teens out and start unloading and pack the stretched passenger van.

As Jack, Jalan and Honest Harry disappear into the small office trailer, Crystal and the drowsy teens spill out of the Jeep and Escort. Micky stumbles out of the Jeep Cherokee and is quickly awestruck by a souped-up '77 Plymouth Duster sitting pretty in the front row. Micky needs a closer look at this classic beauty. Micky's love of cars seem to always put him in hot water. That was the case about two years ago when he stole a neighbor's car in Jersey City to get away from his abusive stepfather. Well, that's the story he'd told Jalan when Jalan had picked him up one night at the Service City Truck Stop about a year ago. This morning Micky's fascination with cars is getting him in trouble with Crystal. She yells, "Micky, get your butt back over here!"

Crystal points to the lengthy church van and directs, "Guys, let's get all of our stuff out and pack up the long van at the end down there."

With a lit cigarette dangling from her fingers, Shelly looks a little nauseated as she steps behind the Canadays' rental, bows her head and leans over. Shelly coughs as if she's vomiting but nothing comes up. She straightens her posture then joins the rest in unloading the cars. Crystal looks at

Shelly taking a drag from her cigarette with a concerned expression but keeps silent.

Toting a small jean bag, multi-pierced and tattooed Josie is anxious to see the van taking them to California. Slyly, Josie sneaks over to the lengthy van. Standing alone alongside the old church carrier, Josie digs out a tube of glossy red lipstick from her small jean purse then scribbles over the faded white paint that'd originally covered the black lettering.

Crystal spots Josie standing near the church van and yells, "Josie! Can you get over here and help us, please?" Wearing a cynical grin, Josie steps away from the van to join the others unloading Jalan's Jeep and the Canadays' Escort. On the left side of the van are freshly marked, red letters spelling 'WET MATCHES' and a huge red 'X' crossing out two words, CHRISTIAN FELLOWSHIP from the original church title: 'SHALLOW CREEK CHRISTIAN FELLOWSHIP CHURCH.'

Carrying two small luggage bags to the old church van, Crystal stops in mid-step as Josie's fresh lipstick markings catch her eye. Crystal is pissed! Immediately, she calls out, "Josie! Josie! Come here, Josie!"

Josie staggers over next to Crystal. Silently, Crystal looks at the bright red letters on the van then turns her head to eyeball Josie. Nonchalantly, Crystal drops both luggage bags then speedily wipes the red lipstick markings off of the van with the palm of her right hand.

Eying Josie, Crystal scorns, "You're NOT wet matches! You got that, Josie?"

Not totally convinced, Josie half-heartedly nods 'yes.' Still looking at Josie with those strong, determined eyes of hers, Crystal blindly wipes her red-stained palm off on her nice slip-over dress, seemingly unconcerned about the mess.

Ready to go, the teens are sitting in the long, white van. The van's rear doors are open as Jalan, Crystal and Jack safely secure the various bags and packed items for their cross-country journey. Abruptly, Jalan is acting rather peculiar. Jalan inconspicuously eyes Jack and Crystal as if he wants to tell them something. Jalan's face turns suddenly serious as he utters, "Hey, Jack and Crystal, you know, um..I think I should -"

Crystal quickly interjects, "Jalan, we already discussed this so there's no need to bring -"

"But," Jalan interrupts.

Crystal cuts Jalan off again and insists, "Listen, let's just get on the road and get our butts to California. How's that?"

"Sounds like a winner to me," Jack interjects.

Unsuccessful at getting a word in edgewise, Jalan gives up and sighs, "Alright, let's do this."

Jalan takes an unusually long look at the heavily-packed, draw-string laundry bag snuggly tucked in the left corner and then shuts the rear doors.

CHAPTER FOUR

The Journey

The following day, the white, rust-spotted church van is traveling west on Interstate 40 somewhere in Tennessee.

Planted up front, Jack sits behind the wheel with his eyes on the road as Jalan buries his head into a foldout road map.

In the second row, Cole seems to be locked into his own world as he writes into his pad. Crystal looks at Cole, admiring his devotion to his literary side. She leans over closer to Cole, invading his personal space. Surprisingly, Cole hands his writing pad to Crystal, allowing her to read his latest creation. Silently, Crystal nods pleasingly as she reads Cole's words. Cole cracks a smile in response to Crystal's favorable acceptance.

In the third row, Josie is peering out of the window at the green Tennessee hills while Micky gazes at her pompous breasts with mannish eyes. Slyly, Micky slowly glides his hand along the little space between them, sliding upward towards Josie's breasts when Josie suddenly and blindly grasps Micky's traveling hand then slowly redirects and guides it between her thighs. Continually looking out the window, Josie spreads her legs as Micky's hand finds the softness he'd been dreaming about for a long time. Josie never makes eye contact with Micky. She continually peers out the window wearing a blank expression as the Tennessee hills roll by. In the fourth row, donning a puzzled face, Shelly cups her breasts with the palm of her hands. She weighs them and then shakes her head in disbelief at their new-found weight. Robbie is softly picking the strings of his guitar and humming a little melody. Shelly is now searching around her seat and on the floor for something. She doesn't find whatever she's looking for.

She turns around, stretching her body over the seat then reaches for a bag familiar to her from the rear. Somewhat frantically, Shelly fishes out a pack of cigarettes. Now satisfied, Shelly relaxes in her seat then nonchalantly lights a cigarette with a chrome lighter.

Towards the front, in the second row, Crystal is sniffing the air as cigarette smoke begins to invade her air. Crystal doesn't look pleased as she sighs, "Shelly, you're not the only one in this van. Some of us don't want to breathe your smoke."

Reluctantly, Shelly squeezes the burning end of her cigarette with the tips of her fingers then eyes Crystal with deep resentment. "Fuckin' bitch," Shelly softly mumbles.

No one sitting towards the front could make out Shelly's mumbled words but Jalan knows her well enough to know that it wasn't very positive. Jalan slightly turns around and aims his fatherly words towards the back, "Shelly, if you got something constructive to say then say it. Otherwise -"

Shelly rolls her eyes at Jalan then rudely interrupts him, "Yes, Daddy."

Smoothly, Robbie breaks the tension in the air by playing his little ditty slightly louder as his fingers strum a steady rhythm on his six-string.

Micky removes his hand from between Josie's legs as Robbie's groove gets his head bobbing and sparks him to rap, "Here we go-Just call me Micky- Here we go-i like it kinda' sticky."

Josie shoots Micky an evil eye as Robbie's groove continues to fill the air.

"Don't be so nasty," Josie says to Micky.

"Look who's talkin'," Micky replies.

Josie rolls her eyes at Micky then turns her back to him.

Shelly gets hit by Robbie's groove. She begins to bob her head to the catchy beat and starts to rap, "My name is Shelly -Can't even smoke- Gotta getaway-Ain't even a joke-My name is Shelly - Can't even smoke - Gotta get away - Ain't even a joke."

Crystal, Jack and Jalan are smiling amusingly at the teens' growing camaraderie as Robbie keeps up the steady rhythm on his six-string.

Eyes fall upon Josie.

"Okay, Josie, you're next," Jalan utters.

Josie is pouting. She's not in the mood for a playful rap as she displays her displeasure with

Micky by keeping her back turned to him. "Pass," Josie answers.

Crystal taps Cole on his shoulder, signaling him to join in on Robbie's groove with a little rap.

On perfect cue, Cole picks up on Robbie's rhythmic beat and smoothly glides his rap into the catchy melody, "They call me the quiet one - My name is Cole -I'm sick - Gonna die - But I try not to cry - They say - be. positive -and look-for the light - But livin' - with HIV - just ain't right."

Crystal and Jack can't believe what their ears just heard. They are completely stunned. Their mouths drop...eyes widen. The entire van suddenly silences.

Unconcerned with the traffic, Jack slams the brakes! The van comes to a sudden stop as cars and trucks swerve around honking their horns in frustration. Honk! Honk! Honk!

Jack is highly upset as he eases the van towards the right shoulder. Jack wants some answers...an explanation...something as he calls out, "Crystal! Jalan!"

Heated, Jack steps out of the van. He awaits Crystal and Jalan. Crystal and Jalan quietly climb out of the van to join Jack.

Still seated in the van, the teens are extremely quiet with all eyes intensely on Jalan, Jack and

Crystal.

Along the shoulder, Jalan, Jack and Crystal are standing next to their long church van as the busy 1-40 traffic passes by. Jack gives his wife a look as if she was withholding secrets. Crystal rapidly shoots him a look that implies that she's left in the dark just as much as him.

Jack is totally pissed. Jalan sighs as he desperately tries to explain things, "Look, I've been trying to tell you guys this but you never gave me a chance to. You see, the church in Shallow Creek used to fund a teen drop-in center in town, thinkin' that would keep the kids from the truck stop. But when some of the congregation found out that some of the kids were HIV positive the funds just stopped…and they've been tryin' to get rid of us ever since. Luckily, I still had some friends in the church to help me get by."

"So who else is HIV positive besides Cole?" Crystal asks.

Jalan sighs, looks at Jack then at Crystal with much concern about their reaction to his answer,

"Everyone."

Jack steps further away. He can't bear the news. Crystal seems both puzzled and deeply concerned at the same time.

Crystal asks, "How do you monitor and control their T-cell count?"

Jalan leads the way toward the back of the van and says, "Let me show you something."

Crystal follows Jalan. Jack still lingers toward the front, trying his best to keep himself cool- headed as he paces.

Jalan opens the rear doors then retrieves the stuffed, draw-string laundry bag. Jalan loosens the draw-string and spreads the bag open. He gestures Crystal to take a peek inside.

Crystal's eyebrows rise as she observes the multiple bottles of prescription drugs.

Jalan continues to explain, "Miss Middleton owns the drugstore and she still supported me when the other church members wanted us gone." Pointing to certain bottles in the bag, Jalan elaborates, "With these, I was able to keep their T-cells stabilized."

"Jalan, let me talk to Jack alone," Crystal says.

Jalan nods 'okay', shuts the rear doors then walks to the front passenger door. Jalan climbs into the van, leaving Crystal on her own to deal with her hot-headed husband.

From inside the van, the teens are still watching with great intensity.

Crystal slowly walks toward the front of the van to confront her pacing husband.

Suddenly, Robbie starts to play his steady guitar groove as Cole, Shelly, Micky and Josie collectively begin to loudly rap in unison, "They say - be positive - and look - for the light! But livin' - with HIV -just ain't right! They say-be positive - and look - for the light! But livin' like this -just ain't right!"

The teens' loud voices are clearly heard outside the van. Without words or gestures, Crystal and Jack stand in awe at the youthful unity in the van.

Crystal looks at Jack, awaiting some kind of response to the harsh-sudden news. Crystal's eyes are piercing Jack's as she silently pleads to him. Jack is slowly being enthralled.

Seconds later, Jack cracks a smile and quips, "You know, woman, I haven't hated you this much since you made me go to that stupid lingerie party."

Relieved, Crystal sighs then glows radiantly with a huge grin. "I love you so much Jack Canaday. Hm, I betcha really gonna divorce me now, huh?" Crystal teases.

"Yep," Jack quickly replies.

"You gonna leave me anything?" Crystal asks.

"Nope," Jack jokingly answers then suggests, "Com'on, we better get back on the road before this old clunker falls apart."

Zooming vehicles pass by as Jack and Crystal step closer to their rust-stained van.

Crystal and Jack climb back into the chorus-filled van as Shelly, Josie, Micky and Cole continually rap to Robbie's rhythmic guitar beat, "They say - be positive - and look - for the light! But livin' like this -just ain't right!"

❧

Somewhere in Arkansas, off of 1-40 West, sits a small roadside gas mart. Jalan steers the rusty, white van next to the regular unleaded pump. Jalan and Jack step out of the van. Jalan stands next to the gas pump as Jack migrates inside the little store to pay the cashier.

Inside the van, the teens look agitated and fidgety as Crystal calmly sits.

"Can we get something to eat here?" Robbie asks.

"Not here. Our next meal stop is later tonight in Tulsa. Just hold your appetite," Crystal answers.

Behind Crystal's back, all of the teens sigh in frustration. Josie has a little difficulty restraining her thoughts as she softly mumbles, "Next meal stop? Like this 'fuckin' Greyhound an' shit."

There's a brief moment of silence then Shelly begins to make quick glances at the others, signaling them with her eyes to follow her lead.

Getting up, Shelly says, "Um, I think I'm just gonna browse and stretch my legs a little bit."

Chubby Robbie is quick to follow Shelly's cue, "I'm gonna stretch my legs too."

"Yeah, me too," Josie adds.

Micky and Cole follow the rest out of the van. One-by-one, the teens crawl out.

Crystal sits silently and patiently in her seat.

Lead by Shelly, who's wearing a slight-mischievous grin, the teens stroll into the tiny mart, passing Jack as he exits the store.

Inside the small-but-plentiful mart, a jolly, heavyset lady stands behind the cash register. The cashier's cheerful, happy-go-lucky face suddenly stiffens and turns to shock.

Awestruck, the cashier's eyes widen while gazing at Shelly's uncombed purple hair, Josie's gang- styled tattoos and silver rings in her pierced nostrils, lower lip and left eyebrow.

The jolly cashier double-takes at the girls then squints her eyes while glancing out the window to take another look at the words on the side of the van. Once again, the cashier's face becomes baffled and confused as she softly reads the black lettering on the side of the lengthy van, "Shallow Creek Christian Fellowship Church."

Abruptly, the lady cashier shakes off her disbelief then utters to the colorful teens, "That's the thing 'bout the Good Lord. He don't care what color your hair is or where you put your jewelry.

He loves everybody...Y'all sang in a choir or some'em?"

The teens smile amusingly at the fat lady's comments but offer no greeting or response as they all disappear down the aisle behind tall racks and shelves of various junk food goodies.

Moments later, one-by-one, with no purchases, Cole, Micky, Josie, Shelly and Robbie quietly stroll out of the store... never making eye contact with the cashier.

With sincere Southern charm, the jolly cashier says, "Didn't like anything, huh? Well, y'all kids enjoy yo'selves while y'all here in Arkansas, alright?"

No one responds.

Patiently, Jalan sits behind the wheel as Jack and Crystal silently watch the teens crawl back into the van and get settled into their seats.

Jalan starts the engine and asks, "Everybody's in?"

Suddenly, Crystal's face turns extremely serious as her eyes zero in on two candy bars protruding from Cole's front pants pocket.

Crystal turns to Jalan and firmly commands, "Cut it off. We're not leaving yet."

Jalan kills the engine as he and Jack exchange glances then they both turn around to see what's bugging Crystal.

The brief silence in the van is broken by the crackling sound of someone opening a bag of chips.

Eying the candy bars sticking out of Cole's pocket and hearing the crackling bag of chips from the rear, Crystal is furious!

"Cole, what's that?" Crystal demands.

Ashamed, Cole doesn't make eye contact with Crystal as he bows his head. Cole is too embarrassed to speak.

"We DON'T STEAL! You guys GOT THAT!" Crystal shouts.

The teens are completely silent as Crystal continually scolds them, "Whatever you guys took I want you to take it back!"

No one moves a muscle. The teens are seemingly frozen stiff in fear of enraged Crystal.

"Now!...MOVE!" Crystal yells.

Hastily, one-by-one, the scorned teens spill out of the van as bags of chips, candy bars, cakes, bags of sunflower seeds and packs of gum dangles from their hands.

Totally fired up, Crystal storms Out of the van, following the teens back into the tiny mart.

Quietly sitting in the van, Jalan glances at Jack with a raised eyebrow.

"She can get pretty spunky, huh?" Jalan utters.

"Aw, that's nothing. You should've seen her once when I used one of her- as she calls them - dinner shoes as a door stopper. Man, my ears hurt for days!" Jack shares.

Amused, Jalan grins.

Inside the store, standing sternly with folded arms near the cashier counter, Crystal eyeballs each teen as they, one-at-a-time, place the junk food they'd stolen atop the counter. Cole and Josie quickly place their stolen goods upon the counter. The stoutly cashier shakes her head in disbelief as the small pile of candy bars, gum and cakes rapidly grows higher. Robbie dumps two squashed packs of cup cakes and three bags of sunflower seeds atop the counter. "Sorry," Robbie shamefully utters to the cashier.

Micky dumps four bags of Skittles upon the counter.

"Sorry," Micky softly mumbles.

Crystal shoots Micky a look. "I don't think she HEARD you," Crystal insists.

"Sorry," Micky repeats with a clearer voice.

Shelly relinquishes an open bag of chips and two packs of Reeses' Pieces atop the counter.

Crystal and the jolly cashier both glance at the open bag of chips then glance at one another.

Crystal feels obligated to pay for the opened bag. To Crystal's surprise, the good-hearted cashier graciously says, "Don't worry 'bout it. Those are my favorite chips. Don't tell my boss, but I eat two of those bags everyday...I'll just finish 'em off by the end of my shift."

Crystal nods 'thanks' to the gracious lady then shoots Shelly a look. Crystal is getting fed up with Shelly. "You have some'em to say to this kind lady, Shelly?" Crystal asks. Shelly rolls her eyes at Crystal then half-heartedly apologizes to the cashier, "Sorry." The long-faced teens solemnly shuffle out of the store as Crystal sighs in disappointment at their behavior. She looks at the cashier and says, "I'm really sorry. They're not bad kids." Puzzled, the cashier asks, "What kinda' church y'all belong to anyway? Is it a good church?" Amused at the cashier's perception that the teens are actually members of a church, Crystal cracks a smile then ponders momentarily.

"Yes, it's a good church. It's a church of second chances," Crystal replies.

"Hm," the cashier utters.

❧

At a roadside diner on the outskirts of Tulsa, the night lights illuminate the dusky Oklahoma sky. The old Chevy Carrier van is parked upfront near the diner's entrance. Directly across the street, Jack exits the lobby of the Tulsa Inn with a handful of room keys.

Inside the diner, sitting around a large oval table, the hungry teens savagely devour plates of bountiful food as Jalan and Crystal stare in complete disbelief. The silverware atop the table is untouched...still neatly wrapped in folded napkins. Some of the wait staff are glancing And sharing looks as the teens use their'hands to shove food into their mouths.

Jack enters and joins the group at the table. Jack flops the hotel room keys atop the table as he takes his place beside Crystal. Immediately, Jack is also taken aback by the seemingly undomesticated youths sharing their table.

"You guys do have forks and spoons, you know," Crystal says.

Chewing, Robbie replies, "Mmmmggeewhhammn." While chewing, Shelly agrees with whatever Robbie just said, "Llllmmmvvviiooofffeemm." Crystal throws her hands into the air while shaking her head in disbelief. She sighs, "Forget it."

Jack, Crystal and Jalan begin to dig into their food. Jalan cuts his roast beef while taking peeks at Shelly.

"Hey, Shelly, Oklahoma City is our next stop. We should be there sometime tomorrow...depends on how early we leave the hotel in the morning. You wanna stop by and say hello to your mom?" Jalan asks.

Instantly, Shelly responds by shaking her head 'no' while simultaneously speaking with a mouthful offood, "Mmm II ain't mm got mm no mama."

Crystal is taken aback by Shelly's remark. Crystal interjects, "Shelly, I'm sure your mother would love to see you again."

Shelly totally ignores Crystal as she shoots Jalan an evil eye for bringing up this subject. Shelly chews and swallows her food. Defiantly, she continues to eyeball Jalan then utters, "It'll be a mistake. Me an' my mom ain't like other moms an' daughters. We ain't like that."

Crystal interjects, "Jalan, do you know where she lives?"

Shelly eyes Crystal with great resentment.

"Yeah, Shelly once spoke of a trailer park on a Euclid Street, I think," Jalan replies.

Donning a triumphant smile, Crystal says, "Good. It'll be fun."

Pissed off, Shelly mocks Crystal's posture and somewhat prissy demeanor. Mimicking Crystal's voice, Shelly says, "Good. It'll be fun."

Shelly picks up her dinner roll from her plate and fires it at Jalan.

"I hate you!" Shelly sneers. In protest, Shelly quickly rise from the table to leave. As she stands, a sharp pain shoots through her stomach. Inconspicuously, Shelly tightens her stomach muscles to ease the pain while concealing her contorting face with a rapid turn from the table. Shelly heads straight for the ladies' room.

Crystal looks at Jalan with a curious face.

"She'll be alright. She's a tough one," Jalan utters.

Crystal nods agreeably as the rest of the group scrape up the last bites of food on their plates.

❧

The following day, on the outskirts of Oklahoma City, the rusty, white Chevy van is turning off of Euclid Street then entering the circular driveway of a small mobile home park. Mail boxes are posted at the edge of each trailer's front lawn. The residents' names and trailer number are boldly visible on the mail boxes.

Jack is behind the wheel. Crystal and Jalan are glancing at each trailer as they pass by and periodically peeking at Shelly to see if she'll help them easily locate her mother's trailer. Shelly rolls her eyes at both Crystal and Jalan. Right now, Shelly wishes to be anywhere but here. Jalan turns to Crystal and suggests, "Just look for a Lori Vincent, I think."

Shelly gives Jalan a look then says, "I don't even know why I even tell ya' things. All you do is blab it to everybody else! I got no privacy and NOBODY wants to listen to MY side!"

Shelly's outburst is momentarily overshadowed as Crystal excitedly points out trailer nine with 'L. Vincent' on its mail box.

"There it is!" Crystal happily says. Jack pulls over and parks the van curbside at trailer nine.

A meaty Honda 750 motorcycle, ornamented with hefty leather saddlebags and shiny chrome pipes, is parked near the trailer's front steps.

Crystal is easing her way out of the van. "Com'on, Shelly," Crystal says. "Why don't you go alone. You're the one who wants to see her - not me," Shelly replies.

Jalan turns around and gives Shelly a look. Shelly certainly knows this particular look. She sighs. In a deep, fatherly tone, Jalan insists, "Shelly, go with Crystal." Reluctantly, Shelly crawls out of the van.

Crystal and Shelly are walking towards the front door. Through the side of her mouth, Shelly says to Crystal, "You better not say a fuckin' word 'bout the HIV thing either."

Crystal is bothered by Shelly's tone and choice of words but shakes it-off for now as they reach the door. Crystal knocks on the door. Appearing at the door is a burly, long-bearded, tattooed man.

"Hi, is there a Lori Vincent here?" Crystal asks.

The hairy gentleman turns his head and let loose a loud call, "Babe! Got company!"

Crystal and Shelly hear a lady's voice asking, "Who is it?"

Crystal tells the tattooed man standing in the doorway, "My name is Crystal and this is -"

"Don't say my name!" Shelly rudely interrupts.

Answering the lady in the house, the burly biker yells back, "Some lady named Crystal and a purple-hair girl named 'Don't say my name'!"

The husky gentleman steps away from the doorway. Seconds later, Thirty-five year old Lori Vincent appears in the doorway. Lori's thinning hair and rotting front teeth makes her look much older than her actual age. Two toddlers are clinging to Lori's legs. Lori's eyes nearly jump out of their sockets after squinting to zero in on the familiar face of the purple-hair girl. "Shell? That you, Shell?" Lori asks. Crystal stands silent and a little dazed at the lukewarm reception. Shelly doesn't respond. She never makes eye contact with her mother. Neither Shelly nor Lori looks happy to see one another. Abruptly, Lori swats her two toddlers off of her legs, "Y'all get now! Go watch TV!" The two kids quickly scatter away. Lori turns to Shelly and asks, "Who's this? Yo' probation officer?"

Crystal is shocked at Lori's perception of her. Eying Shelly with a cold stare, Lori seems upset and needs to let off some pent-up steam, "Why the hell ya' come back now? You wanna take my man? Fuckin' funny how ya' just happen to show up when I find somebody decent! You ain't bringin' yo' ass here! An' why ya' paintin' yo' hair purple? Ain't no use in hidin' yo'self behind all that purple hair...You ain't gonna be nuddin' but po' white trash like yo' mama, girl - So stop tryin' to be some'em ya' ain't!"

Lori's eyes squints tighter as they. zero in on Shelly's slightly bloated stomach.

"Is that a trick baby?" Lori asks.

Stunned, Crystal leans forward to take a peek at Shelly's stomach. Shelly has had enough. She turns around...heads back to the van without a word or a wave goodbye.

Crystal is left alone with Lori. The moment is awkward and silent until Crystal utters, "She's your daughter and we were only hoping -

"Look, I don't know whatcha got goin' wit' Shell an' all but the bottom line is sometimes blood just ain't thicker than water," Lori interrupts.

Lori steps back inside the trailer, leaving Crystal completely dumbfounded as she tries to absorb the harsh reality of Shelly's life.

Moments later, Crystal joins the rest in the van.

Crystal crawls into the van. Facing her past is the hardest thing Shelly's ever done. Her tough skin can't seem to protect her from this. Shelly is fighting back tears and begins to sniffle as she sits somberly beside Robbie.

Looking at Jack, Crystal says, "Let's get outta here. But make sure you stop at the first drugstore you see."

As the van pulls away, Shelly's sniffling has turned into all-out sobbing. Jalan turns around to check on Shelly as she blindly leans her head upon Robbie's shoulder. Awkwardly, Robbie stiffens. He's never been in this type of circumstance before. Jalan looks at Robbie in disbelief. "Hold her, Robbie! Put your arms around her!" Jalan orders.

Awkwardly, Robbie's stiffen arms begin to straighten out as they flop down upon Shelly's sobbing, heartbroken body.

&

The long Carrier van is parked near the front entrance of a suburban drugstore. Inside, at the checkout line, Crystal places a pregnancy kit upon the conveyor belt as Shelly sighs. The cashier scans the pregnancy kit and Crystal pays cash. Excitedly, Crystal asks, "Is there a restroom we can use?"

Shelly sighs again as the cashier kindly points to a set of green doors along the right wall. Crystal hastily drags a somewhat reluctant Shelly to the ladies' room.

Minutes later, standing outside the ladies' room, Jalan, Jack, Micky, Josie, Cole and Robbie are awaiting the big news. Both Jalan and Jack look somewhat worrisome. Robbie, Cole and Micky looks like they'd rather be elsewhere.

Finally, the door swings open. Surprised to see everyone, Crystal's mouth drops. Shelly dons her usual nonchalant look as they face the rest of the gang in the hallway.

"So is she or what?" Josie asks.

Crystal lets the anticipation build a little then replies, "Yes!"

Immediately, Jack and Jalan sigh in disappointment as great concern begin to sink in.

Overwhelmed and upset by the news, Jalan walks away. Jack eyes Crystal as she maternally wraps her warms around Shelly's shoulders. Micky, Cole and Robbie are frozen... unsure of how to react to the news.

Josie turns to the boys and says, "Get happy, dudes. You shitheads gonna be fuckin' uncles!" The boys still stand around looking somewhat perplexed. Jack slowly walks closer to Crystal and Shelly. Both Crystal and Jack realize the seriousness of this news. They have different concerns but manage to convey their support of one another through their eyes.

In a warm sisterly way, Josie gives Shelly a hug.

"I'm tellin' you right now - I ain't changin' no diapers," Josie teases.

As the group walks out of the store, Shelly looks out the window at Jalan standing solemnly alone next to the van. Through the corner of her eyes, Crystal notice Shelly looking at the only real father-figure she'd ever known.

Reassuringly, Crystal tells Shelly, "Give Jalan some time. In time, he'll accept this."

Ω

The old church van is traveling along a lonesome stretch of highway through Texas' flat, barren landscape. Jack is behind the wheel. It's late in the evening and, seemingly, everyone else is asleep except for Micky who's seated in the third row.

Micky looks totally bored as he gazes at the monotonous Texas scenery.

Jack glances into the rearview mirror. He notice a wide awake Micky in the midst of sleeping bodies. Jack slows the van to a snail's pace then softly whispers to Micky, "Hey Micky, wanna drive?"

Jack steers the van to the shoulder then slowly stops. Gesturing to Micky to be as quiet as possible, Jack slides out of the driver seat then stoops uncomfortably between the two front seats as Micky sneakingly exits the side door then quietly slides into the driver seat.

Inconspicuously, Crystal, who's lying down in the second row, peeks at Jack. Silently, she cracks a smile while peeping at her husband acting like a proud father to Micky.

Like a pro, Micky seems to be very comfortable and at ease behind the wheel as Jack closely
monitors his every move.

"Micky, you can't tell the others 'bout this, okay?" Jack softly says.

Amused, Crystal widens her smile at her sneakish husband then shuts her eyes...pretending to

be asleep.

Micky carefully steers the van along the lonesome 1-40 West as Jack keeps close watch.

*

The next day, the rust-spotted van is in the flow of light traffic. A roadside sign boasts...

WELCOME TO NEW MEXICO

Other than Jack and Jalan switching driving duties periodically, the seating arrangements have remained the same throughout the trip.

Upfront, Jalan is now behind the wheel as Jack takes a much-needed nap.

In the second row, Cole is bobbing his head to the cool sounds pumping in from his walkman while simultaneously jotting down words into his writing pad. Somewhat bored, Crystal playfully glances at Cole's writing pad. Catching Crystal stealing peeks at his more-private material, Cole slightly turns his pad from Crystal's view. Again, Crystal playfully leans over, stretching her neck to get a better view.

In the third row, Micky's hand slides gently between Josie's thighs as she gaze out the window wearing a blank expression. By the look on Micky's gleaming face he thinks he's in heaven.

In the fourth row, Robbie is fiddling with his six-string. Shelly looks totally bored as she stares out the window at New Mexico's rocky, empty terrain.

Moments later, Shelly leans forward and reaches on the floor between her feet to retrieve a pack of cigarettes from a plastic bag. She fishes out her chrome lighter from her jeans.

Concerned, Robbie glances at Shelly then gives her a look. Shelly turns face-to-face with Robbie and places a finger across her lips, "SSsssshhh."

Robbie shakes his head in disbelief at Shelly's gutsiness. Shelly lowers her head, hiding behind the seat in front of her as she fires up a cigarette.

In the second row, Crystal's nose begins to twitch as she curiously glances around. It doesn't take Crystal long to find the source of the smoky smell.

Crystal yells, "Jalan, stop the van!"

Crystal's alarming voice wakes Jack. Jalan quickly slows the van and eases off of the highway.

"Shelly, what did I tell you about those cigarettes?" Crystal shouts.

'Fuck you! You ain't MY mother!" Shelly defiantly fires back.

The entire van falls silent as Crystal begins to crawl out and firmly commands, "Shelly! Outside NOW!"

Crystal is waiting outside for Shelly's arrival. Reluctantly, Shelly crawls out of the van with the lit cigarette between her fingers. Inside, the van is completely silent as everyone seems to be in shock. Outside, Crystal's right hand wallops against Shelly's surprised face!

"This is gonna stop! You understand me, Shelly?" Crystal shouts.

Crystal snatches the lit cigarette from Shelly's fingers then stomps it out.

"You got anything to say?" Crystal asks.

Submissively, Shelly shakes her head 'no.'

Knowing that things between her and Shelly will be different from this moment forward, Crystal

commandly gets back into the van. Everyone is frozen silent as Shelly crawls in.

Shelly cups her nose with her right hand as a blood streak trickles from her nostril. She sniffles while making her way to her seat.

"And now that you're pregnant, Shelly, no more cigarettes," Crystal says.

While sniffling, Shelly respectfully replies, "Yes, ma'am."

Crystal digs out a small, travel-size packet of tissues from her purse then hands it behind her to

Josie.

"Here, Josie, pass this to Shelly," Crystal says.

Josie takes the mini-pack from Crystal.

"Yes, ma'am," Josie says politely.

Crystal senses the tension still lingering in the air. She doesn't want the teens to be afraid of her... but only to respect her.

Crystal sighs, "You don't have to ma'am me, Josie - You can call me Crystal."

Still a little fearful, Josie responds, "Yes, ma'am."

Amused, Jalan and Jack share smiles.

Ready to hit the road again, Jalan starts the engine then slowly merge back onto the freeway.

From this moment on, not only Shelly, but Josie, Robbie, Micky and Cole will never look at

Crystal the same way again.

At a highway rest area somewhere in Arizona, eighteen wheelers, RV's, a dozen other vehicles, including the rusty church van, are parked in a lengthy parking lot stretched along the right shoulder. The hood is raised on the battered van as steam bellows out from the overheated radiator.

Jalan's at the rear of the van. The back doors are open. Several labeled prescription bottles are balanced atop the draw-string laundry bag. Jalan is meticulously placing particular into five disposable cups.

Numerous travelers are utilizing the rest area's various amenities. A young couple is walking their French terrier in a sectioned-off pet area carpeted with plush, green grass. A family of six is viewing the numerous, encased pictures of

Arizona's scenic wonders proudly gracing the brick walls at the Visitors Center.

Near the Visitors Center entranceway, an old Indian woman is selling authentic Native- American jewelry and other colorful, handmade items.

In the vast picnic section, Jack and Crystal are sitting romantically close at one of several redwood tables. Protected from the sultry Arizona sun, the teens are relaxing on the grass under branchy, shade trees. Micky and Josie are laying dangerously close. Josie is repeatedly removing Micky's left hand off of her legs. Robbie seems to be strumming out a new song on his guitar as he periodically stops to jot down lyrics on a loose piece of paper. Cole is listening to his walkman while writing his thoughts into his pad.

Wearing a peculiar expression, Shelly runs her fingers along her slightly-protruding stomach.

Back at the picnic table, Jack and Crystal are eying the teens a short distance away.

"What are we doing, Crystal?" Jack ponders.

"I don't know, Jack...but it's the right thing," Crystal replies.

Jack nods agreeably while lovingly wrapping his arm around his wife.

Jalan exits the Visitors Center with a half-gallon jug of water then returns to mixing the teens' medicine at the rear of the van.

Minutes later, Jalan joins Jack and Crystal at the table as he carefully places a makeshift cardboard tray loaded with the five drinks atop the table.

Jalan calls out to the teens, "Okay guys, it's ready."

The teens struggle up from the grass then shuffle over to the picnic table. Jack leans over and peeks into the five cups. Jack grimaces, "Man, how in the world do they swallow that stuff?"

"If they wanna live, they have no choice...over time though I did learn to mix an' sweeten it up a lit'l," Jalan replies.

The teens reach the table and methodically grab and swallow the foamy cocktail in the cups. While observing the teens finish the last drop, Jalan instructs, "Until the motor cools, we gonna be here for awhile so stick together an' don't venture off."

The teens nod 'okay' then scatter back underneath the shade trees. While walking away, Shelly glances back at Jalan. Jalan's unaware of her glance. A touch of guilt surfaces upon Shelly's face. She wants to talk to Jalan but can't seem to find the right approach. Shelly shakes the though then eases herself down underneath a leafy shade tree. She softly cups her stomach with her palms.

Robbie resumes his song creation while practicing his new melody on his six-string.

Cole inserts a CD into his walkman then resumes to his literary masterpiece on his pad.

Micky's not wasting any time trying to feel the softness between Josie's legs as they lay closely underneath a thick dogwood. Micky's not having any luck today as Josie constantly ejects his travelling hand.

At the picnic table, Crystal is watching Josie and Micky with a concerned expression. Crystal turns to Jalan and asks, "What's with Josie and Micky?"

Jalan sighs, "Um, how can I put this?...One day my man Mick is gonna get his heart broken. You see, Josie likes the same thing he likes - if you know what I mean - but she haven't told him yet." Jack and Crystal's eyebrows rise as Jalan continues to elaborate on certain events that took place in Josie's past. When Jalan first met Josie at the truck stop she was mean and scared. It took her quite awhile to trust him and share things with him. One night, at the rundown shack in the woods, Jalan saw Josie crying all alone and when he went over to comfort her that's when she'd told about her last night in Jersey. Jalan goes on and explains to Jack and Crystal that about two years ago tattooed Josie was on a worn out sofa in an old, abandon apartment building locking lips with a sensuous female friend who she'd been secretly seeing for about three weeks. Suddenly, the door swings open. Six members from Josie's gang enter. Josie was as surprised as they were. She thought that they'd be gone for another couple hours due to some party across town. But it was raided so they went back to their hangout. Fear began to spread across Josie's face as she quickly scooted and tried to distance herself from her sexy, young friend. Awkwardly, Josie tried to pretend that nothing sexual was going on between them but her gang members weren't fooled. At first, the six heavily-tattooed gangsters glance at one another with a bit of confusion, and then cold, menacing stares shot across the room. Josie and her curvaceous friend hastily struggled up from the sofa then quickly stepped toward the door to leave. Immediately, the six roughneck gangsters closed ranks, blocking Josie's path.

After learning how Josie was beaten and chased out of Jersey by her old street gang, Crystal ponders then asks Jalan, "She got any family?"

"Sure do. Me, you, Jack, Shelly, Robbie, Cole and Mick," Jalan quickly answers.

Both Crystal and Jack nod agreeably.

Approximately an hour later, Jack, Crystal, Jalan, Shelly, Micky, Josie and Robbie are all asleep underneath the shade trees. Seemingly, Cole is nowhere in sight.

Micky and Josie are lying next to each other under the thick dogwood. A folded sheet of paper slightly moves as it balances upon Micky's forehead. Abruptly, a tiny twig falls from the branches above then hits the folded paper resting atop Micky's forehead. Startled, Micky awakes! Baffled, Micky swats the folded paper off of his forehead! Looking around, Micky finds everyone asleep then he double-takes at the empty spot underneath the tree where Cole was earlier. Micky realizes that Cole's gone! Sincerely concerned, Micky's face turns deadly serious. Micky reaches for the folded sheet of paper then frantically unfolds it. Micky hastily reads the handwritten words on the paper, "I tried to find myself with you all but it seems like I just don't fit anywhere. I would like to thank you all for trying to help me but I think it's time for me to go now. Good luck in California. Cole." Hysterically, Micky drops the note then, at the top of his lungs, alarms, "Wake up! Cole's gone! Everybody wake up! Cole's gone!"

Startled, everyone struggles up...looking at Micky as he echoes his resounding alarm, "Cole's gone !"

Suddenly, one of the thick dogwood branches begin to shake then Cole drops down, landing next to hysterical Micky!

Everyone except for Micky erupts into chuckles and laughter as Cole coolly turns toward Micky.

"Yo Micky, I just had to see if you had any love for me, that's all," Cole explains.

"Damn! Couldn't ya' just ask me? Damn!" Micky yells.

Cole coolly walks away with a huge grin stretched across his face, knowing that Micky truly

cares for him. Micky is embarrassed as the rest of the gang continually laughs and chuckles.

An hour later, Jalan is out in the parking lot checking under the van's raised hood. Jalan steps away from the van shaking his head in frustration. Apparently, the engine still hasn't cooled down enough. Shelly is approaching Jalan. She looks as though something is weighing heavy on her mind.

Somewhat nervously, Shelly asks, "Can I talk to you for a minute, Jalan?"

Jalan stands with his arms folded, sighs then gives Shelly his undivided attention.

Choking on her words at times, Shelly begins to vent, "Look, I know you told us not to go back to the truck stop no more an' stuff but nobody else was givin' me cigarettes an' stuff and then..um, I guess..an' well.you know how some of 'em guys don't wanna use a condom."

Jalan sighs then struggles to maintain his composure as Shelly, who's fighting back tears now, continues, "I know you're mad at me but I just wanna say that I'm sorry if I disappointed you or hurt you and I..I..um probably don't show it good but I love you very much an' you're the only Daddy I ever had..an' if I have a boy I'm gonna name him Jalan."

Touched by Shelly's words, Jalan breaks his stance and invites Shelly into his forgiving open arms. Relieved, Shelly melts as she lays her head upon his chest.

"Shelly, please understand that I am bothered a little that you're havin' a trick baby but, honestly, my main concern now is that we do all that's medically possible to have a healthy baby without being HIV positive...And other than that, girl, I do consider you my daughter," Jalan reassuringly says.

"For real!" Shelly blissfully cheers as she tightens her hug around Jalan.

Jalan flashes a proud father smile

❧

At a picnic table, Crystal and Josie are having a private moment alone.

"You like being a White girl?" Josie asks.

Josie's uncanny question catches Crystal off-guard. Crystal is completely taken aback.

"I never really thought about it...1 don't know...1 think so," Crystal answers.

"You're kinda' tough for a White girl," Josie says.

Unsure of how to respond, Crystal smiles amusingly then utters, "Thanks, Josie...Thanks."

There's a brief moment of silence then Crystal asks, "Now 'bout you? Do you like who you are,
Josie?"

Smiling, Josie replies, "Sometimes."

Underneath a shade tree, Jack is listening to Robbie play his guitar. Wearing a pleased expression, Jack is impressed with the soft, melodic tune.

As Robbie plays his guitar sometimes he escapes and lets his music take him places. Right now, as his soft melody fills the air, Robbie's mind drifts back a year ago when chubby Robbie was doing his usual chores in the barn on the family farm in Stafford, Virginia. Robbie begins to fork a pile of hay, shuffling it up to mix the wet strands with the dry. The barn door is slightly open. A slither of sunlight illuminates the barn inside. Abruptly, the barn darkens. Robbie becomes nervously stiff as an older farmhand slips through the barn door then calmly closes it. Robbie quickly tosses his pitchfork aside then tries to hide behind a tractor parked near the left corner of the barn. Robbie is easily forced on all fours! His pants are yanked off! Robbie tries to hastily crawl away, digging his fingers frantically into the damp soil, but is quickly manhandled as his underwear is yanked down to his ankles! The overpowering farmhand swiftly straddles Robbie's exposed backside... As Robbie's mind continues to drift, he's running through thick underbrush and a wooded area then stops after reaching his refuge...his sanctuary at a clearance along the bank of a slow-moving river. Robbie sits on a log, hangs his head and begins to cry.

Jack is bobbing his head to Robbie's catchy beat. He's truly impressed by Robbie's talent.

"Wow Robbie, that's really good. You make up your own songs? Got words to this one yet?"

Jack asks.

Robbie's not responding to Jack. Momentarily, Robbie seems deeply gone into his own world.

"Hey Robbie, 'you okay?" Jack asks.

"I'm sorry. I kinda' lose it sometimes," Robbie says.

"I really like that one. You do your own stuff, huh?" Jack repeats.

"I'm still workin' on the lyrics though. It's gonna be called Rappahannock Dreams," Robbie replies.

"Hm. What it's about?" Jack asks.

Robbie isn't used to someone asking him about his music. Robbie seems on-guard.

"You really wanna know?" Robbie asks.

"Sure," Jack quickly replies.

Robbie is hesitant at first, but slowly begins to do something that he hasn't done in quite while. With water building in his eyes, Robbie explains, "It's about this sad boy who used to hang out near this river and just dream that the water could just take him away from all his troubles and problems." Tears begin to streak down Robbie's face. Jack realizes that this new song of Robbie's is actually about Robbie himself so he figures that this could be a good moment to pick Robbie's spirit up by sharing something personal from his life.

Somewhat awkwardly, Jack utters, "Robbie, I'm not that good with words and all...but um...when I was twelve a bunch of Black boys did something real bad to me and I thought I would hate Black guys all my life...and then I met Jalan and Micky."

Robbie looks a little confused. "Jack, I don't know if you noticed or not but I'm a fat White guy so -"

"The point is Robbie...um...um," Jack interrupts but awkwardly still can't seem to find the proper words. "Well, Robbie, just keep...um...playing that guitar. That's it. Just keeping playing that guitar," Jack sighs.

Puzzled, Robbie replies, "Oh, oookay."

Minutes later, Crystal and the five teens are at the pet area admiring a cute poodle as its owner allows the teens to pat and hold it. Several yards away, Jalan and Jack are having a guy-moment at the picnic table.

"I was just tellin' Robbie how I'd never thought that I'd ever have a Black buddy," Jack shares.

Amused, Jalan grins.

"We're buddies, Jack?" Jalan asks.

Jack extends his hand for a shake. Jalan gladly shakes Jack's hand.

Jack reiterates, "Buddies."

Jack has never had the best timing. Once he gets something on his mind it sort of just comes out. This is one of those times. Suddenly, Jack turns somewhat serious.

"Um, you and Crystal ever...ever...you know?" Jack awkwardly asks.

Jalan begins to grow a sinister grin, as if he's up to something.

"Jack, there's one thing I'd learned in life - Don't ever ask a woman about her sexual history," Jalan offers.

Jalan glances at Crystal and the teens several yards away at the pet area.

Jalan loudly calls, "Hey, Crystal, come here for a minute."

Jack looks worried. Jalan is grinning.

"Whatcha doing?" Jack nervously asks.

"Jack, I can't pass this one up. It's too easy. You betta' say a prayer 'cause you're in some hot water now, dude," Jalan says.

Crystal comes over to the table. Jack stiffens.

Jalan looks at Crystal with a straight face and nonchalantly says, "Jack and I was talkin' and Jack um...Jack wants to know if we'd ever slept together."

Immediately, Crystal's face turns furious as she looks at Jack. Jalan smiles while trying his best to retain his laughter. Crystal glances at Jalan and utters, "Aw, no he didn't." She quickly eyeballs her husband and bluntly asks, "Did you?"

Consumed with guilt, Jack offers no response.

Abruptly, Crystal shoves Jack with all of her might! Jack tumbles over then rolls upon the ground! Crystal towers over him, daring him to get up with her piercing eyes!

"Did I EVER ask you did you screw Wanda? Carol? Becky? Linda? Vickie? NO!" Crystal yells.

While taking a verbal beating from his heated wife, Jack shoots grinning Jalan an evil eye. Jack needs to find a way to get rid of his newfound, instigating buddy.

"Hey Jalan, the motor's probably cool enough now. Won'tcha go make yourself useful and check it out so we can get outta this place," Jack suggests.

Crystal's not through with Jack yet. She gives him a look then shakes her head in disbelief,

"Jack, I can't believe you asked him that."

Shamefully, Jack replies, "I didn't mean t -"

"Oh just shut up, Jack," Crystal interrupts.

Wearing a huge grin, Jalan steps away to check on the van's motor then briefly looks back at

Jack and teases, "Hey Jack, we're still buddies, right?"

Crystal looks down at her husband. A loving smile slowly evolves on Crystal's face as Jack struggles up off of the ground.

"Jack Canaday. if you wasn't so damn lovable I'd dump you," Crystal says.

"Hey, I'm really not THAT lovable, you know. And I haven't been single in awhile so let's go for it," Jack teases.

"Shut up, Jack," Crystal quickly utters with a look.

CHAPTER FIVE

New Home, New Beginnings

It's been a long cross-country journey for the Canadays, Jalan and the teens. They've finally reached Seaside, California. The old Chevy van is travelling along picturesque Oceanview Lane, passing towering lollipop palm trees on both sides. The awe-inspiring, blue waving waters of the Pacific Ocean can be seen in the short distance ahead. Behind the wheel, Jalan is glancing around in amazement at the beautiful scenery as Jack points and guides him towards their new home at 1511 Oceanview Lane.

In the back of the van, everyone else is soundly asleep. The lengthy trip has brought the entire gang closer together. Cole is stretched out across the seat with his head resting upon Crystal's legs. Sleeping with her head leaning against the window, Crystal's arms are running across Cole's face. Josie's legs are resting across Micky's knees. In the final row, Shelly is comfortably nestled across Robbie's lap as his arms softly lay atop her shoulders.

Nearing the Canadays' home, Jack turns around and alarms, "Wake up, guys! We're home!" A short distance ahead, the two-story, luxurious house at 1511 Oceanview Lane comes into view. Jack gestures Jalan to pull into the paved, circular driveway as the waking teens look out the windows in complete awe at the lollipop palm trees and ocean blue water just a couple of blocks away. Robbie's eyes widen and mouth drops.

"Is this where we 'gonna be livin' now?" Robbie asks.

"This is home, Robbie," Crystal answers.

"Wow," Robbie utters.

❧

Everyone is spilling out of the old church van. Micky is immediately awestruck by Jack's red Toyota Pathfinder and the glossy black Jaguar with the vanity plates 'CRYSTAL' parked in the driveway. Wide-eyed with envy, Micky strolls over to the shiny red Pathfinder to take a closer look. Cole is mesmerized by the cool sea breeze and incredible ocean view.

"Can we go to the beach after we unload?" Cole excitedly asks. "Yeah! Let's go check out the babes!" Micky interjects.

While retrieving bags from the rear of the van, Jack turns to Crystal and says, "Honey, after we're done me and the guys are gonna go check out babes...Cool?"

Amused, Crystal cracks a smile at Jack's playful mood and decides to play along, "Cool."

"You know, you're such an understanding wife. I think I'm gonna keep you after all," Jack quips.

"Cool," Crystal says.

Donning a look of admiration as she briefly toys with her husband's hair, Crystal notices and appreciates Jack's more-relaxed attitude since taking their cross-country journey.

As everyone helps to unload the van, Shelly pulls Jalan aside for a private talk.

"Can I borrow ten bucks? I promise to pay you back," Shelly pleads.

Without hesitation, Jalan fishes out his wallet and pinches out a ten dollar bill. He hands it to

Shelly.

"Remember, no more cigarettes," Jalan says.

"No, this is for some'em way more important than cigarettes...Thanks," Shelly says.

‿⁀

An hour later, steady ocean waves rush the sandy shore as scantily clad beach goers enjoy the California sun. Pedestrians stroll along the lengthy, wooden pier as the graceful seagulls hover and effortlessly float above. Several beach bars line the coast as hand-painted sandwich boards advertise their happy hours and open mike nights.

Micky, Cole, Robbie, Jalan and Jack are strolling along the sandy shoreline. Cole's face illuminates as he eyes a young lady wearing a sexy bikini while writing into her notepad.

She's lying on her side atop a colorful beach towel. Micky notices Cole staring at the young lady.

"Go get her phone number, Cole," Micky suggests.

Cole looks back at Jack and Jalan, asking them for their opinion through his eyes.

"Go for it," Jack says.

"You're the man," Jalan cheers.

Cole shakes his shoulders, straightens his posture then walks over towards the young lady as she continually scribbles into her writing pad. From a short distance away, the rest of the guys watch Cole's every move with sports-like anticipation.

Cole nervously approaches the lady and accidently steps on the young lady's toes. She gestures to him that she's okay. It seems as though that Cole and the young lady are hitting it off. She smiles and allows him to penetrate her personal space by gesturing him to bend down to take a closer look at the words on her notepad. Seconds later, the young lady is jotting down her phone number on a piece of paper then handing it to Cole.

Cole turns around with a look of disbelief. He can't believe that he actually pulled it off. Seconds later, Cole kisses the piece of paper and walks away wearing a triumphant grin. Micky, Robbie, Jack and Jalan start to high-five one another as Cole nears. "You're the man!" Jalan boasts.

As the guys continue their walk along the beach, Robbie eyes a beach bar sandwich board advertising, 'OPEN MIKE NITE - TONIGHT AT 7 PM.' Robbie leans closer to Micky then whispers something into his ear.

Meanwhile, back at the house, Crystal is showing Shelly and Josie the nursery room that she'd been working on for the past year. Crystal and the girls are standing around the toy-filled crib as bright colored animals of the mobile dangle above.

"Finally, we can put this room to use," Crystal says.

Josie is admiring all of the colorful stuffed animals in the crib.

Shelly looks at Crystal with apologetic eyes then begins to dig out the ten dollar bill from her jean shorts.

"Crystal, here. I owe you this, remember?" Shelly utters.

Taken aback, Crystal accepts the ten dollar bill from Shelly's hand.

"You're a good girl, Shelly...Thanks," Crystal says.

Wearing a puzzled face, Josie looks at Shelly and asks, "Where's my ten?"

Shelly offers a blank expression.

"Oh, I see, I guess it's a White thing, huh? Well, 'cuuuusse me," Josie teases.

❧

Later in the evening, Jack, Crystal and Jalan are hanging new curtains and placing a small three-drawer desk into the right corner of Jalan's new room.

Momentarily, Jalan takes a step back just to observe his new room as Crystal and Jack continue to tidy things up.

"I don't know how I could ever repay you guys," Jalan says.

"Are you any good with a hammer?" Jack asks.

Not giving Jalan a chance to answer, Crystal quickly slaps Jack on his arm then scorns, "Jack!"

She turns to Jalan with warm, inviting eyes and says, "You don't owe us a cent. This is home...And I'd already set up a meeting with my boss. We could use some help at the clinic."

"Great," Jalan replies. Jack notices the silence throughout the house.

"Listen," Jack says while gesturing to Crystal and Jalan. Puzzled, Jalan and Crystal join Jack as they all observe the complete silence.

"You're right. It's way too quiet. I'll go check on them," Crystal says as she leaves the room. Two minutes later, Crystal returns and alarms, "They're all gone! And the Pathfinder's gone also!"

"Micky!" Jack assumes. Not wasting any time, Jack dash out of the room. Hastily, Jalan and Crystal follow close behind.

A short time later, at the beach bar, Micky, Josie, Shelly and Cole are sitting at the closest table to the tiny, platform stage where chubby Robbie sits alone upon a bar stool. Robbie looks a little nervous as he fine-tunes the strings on his guitar. The cozy bar is jam packed with a lively crowd. The emcee steps onto the small stage and stands next to Robbie. Unbeknownst to the teens, Jack, Crystal and Jalan enter the bar. Jack spots the teens sitting upfront then gestures Crystal and Jalan. Jack cuts through the crowd and goes straight to Micky's chair. Immediately,

Jack places his hands upon Micky's shoulders. Jack's grasp on Micky's shoulders tightens. Micky knows what he wants. Seconds later, Micky relinquishes the Pathfinder keys. Jack releases his grip. Jalan and Crystal join the teens at the table as all eyes fall upon Robbie. The emcee steps closer to the microphone, "And now, how 'bout a big California welcome for our next performer who tells me that he just got here all the way from Shallow Creek, Virginia...Let's hear it for....RRRRRobbie!

The lively crowd erupts with applause. Robbie begins to strum his guitar as a soft melody fills the air and the crowd falls silent, giving Robbie their undivided attention. Robbie continues to play the soft melody while introducing his song, "I like to do a new song I wrote. It's called Rappahannock Dreams."

The crowd is captivated by Robbie's musical talent as his fingers easily glide over the guitar strings, creating a mesmerizing rhythm.

Robbie begins to sing, "Leaves fallin' down and tears in my eyes - I sit by this river and cry and cry-But just like running water-running water-These Rappahannock dreams keep passin' me by - But someday soon I'm gonna get away from here - Just like running water - clear and clear-I sit by this river and cry and cry - Somebody please - please-Tell me why these Rappahannock dreams keep passin' me by."

As Robbie slowly fades his song out, the pleased crowd stands with a rousing applause! Moved by the song, Shelly steps onto the stage to reward Robbie with a warm hug. Josie quickly joins Shelly and plants a tender kiss on Robbie's left cheek.

※

The following day, Cole looks extremely excited as he stuffs his backpack with his writing pad. He's about to leave as Crystal enters the living room donning a curious face.

"Where ya' goin', Cole? And where's everybody else at?" Crystal asks.

"Robbie's been hired at the bar. Shelly an' Josie went for a walk on the beach with the new bikinis you'd bought them. They said that they wanted to see how many heads they could turn. And Jack took Micky to the construction site...Oh, and um Jalan's out back...And you're standin' right there," Cole quickly reports.

Crystal gives Cole a look then says, "You still haven't told me where you're going." Cole unzips his backpack and retrieves his writing pad. He gestures Crystal to come closer.

Showing Crystal the title page of the story that he's been writing, Cole excitedly explains, "This is what I've been workin' on. I'm calling it 'Not Wet Matches', and my friend I'd met at the beach is gonna help me type it all up...And she says that she's gonna help me find a publisher too!"

"I'm impressed. That's really great, Cole...but tell me more about this girl," Crystal says. Cole wants to leave. He stuffs the pad back into his backpack then steps toward the door.

"I gotta go," Cole says.

"Cole's gotta girlfriend, Cole's gotta girlfriend," Crystal teases.

"Now I really gotta go... See ya'," Cole says as he shuts the door.

❦

Crystal walks into the kitchen. She sees Jalan sitting alone on a comfortable lounge chair on the back patio. Crystal peeks in the refrigerator and grabs a picture of lemonade. She pours two glasses and joins Jalan on the back patio.

"Thirsty?" Crystal asks while handing Jalan a tall glass of lemonade. "Thanks," Jalan says.

"Whatcha' thinking about out here? Are you nervous about the meeting at the clinic tomorrow?" Crystal asks.

"I just can't get over how much you and Jack has helped me and the kids," Jalan replies.

"Just all part of the ten thousand people before we die, remember?" Crystal coolly says.

Jalan grins and utters, "Jack's a real lucky dude."

"Yes he is," Crystal smoothly replies.

⸙

Jack is at the construction site happily introducing Micky to Donny and the rest of the crew. Jack notices the Black timid-looking boy hammering nails into a two-by-four a few yards away. Jack pulls Donny aside and asks, "What's the kid's name again from the High School Summer Job Program?"

"That's Kevin Morris. He's workin' out great for us, Boss. He's a real good kid," Donny answers.

Immediately, Jack looks at Micky and gestures him to follow as he heads over towards Kevin. Kevin stops hammering as Jack approaches. "Hey, Kevin, I wanna thank you for doing a great job for us. And if you don't mind, could you show Micky here around and kinda' teach him some stuff?" Jack asks.

A proud smile spreads across Kevin's face as he replies, "Me? ...Sure."

֍

The following day, at the County Health Clinic, Crystal and ponytailed Jalan are sitting across the glossy, oak desk of the clinic's director, Ms. Thompson.

Ms. Thompson wears a no-nonsense expression as she delivers disappointing news to Jalan and Crystal, "Mr. Simms, I'm truly impressed by your resume, and it's amazing what you've done in Virginia with those kids. But, we're a County clinic with limited County funds. Look, we're certainly understaffed but we simply can't afford t-"

"Cut my salary in half," Crystal interrupts.

Ms. Thompson is taken aback as she looks at Crystal with a puzzled expression.

"Cut...my...salary...in...half," Crystal slowly reiterates.

Ms. Thompson is blown away by Crystal's determination. She sits back in her high-back, cushion chair and looks at Crystal with tremendous admiration and respect.

Abruptly, Ms. Thompson turns to Jalan and says, "Mr. Jalan Simms, welcome aboard."

"Thank you," Jalan replies.

As Jalan turns to thank Crystal, she beats him to the punch and coolly gives him a wink.

Meanwhile, out in the lobby and reception area, Shelly, Josie, Micky, Robbie and Cole are handing their intake questionnaire forms to the overworked receptionist behind the counter. There aren't enough chairs for the weary crowd packed into the lobby. Reluctantly, the colorful teens join the others already standing against the walls. Eye-catching posters offering messages about drug prevention, HIV/ AIDS prevention tips, pregnancy prevention and prenatal care grace the lobby walls.

The receptionist thumbs through the teens' five intake questionnaire forms while donning a peculiar, somewhat puzzled face.

Crystal and Jalan are returning from Ms. Thompson's office. Crystal leads Jalan from the lengthy corridor into the busy lobby area.

The receptionist notices Crystal entering the lobby. She gestures and says, "Hey, Crystal, come here. You gotta see this." Crystal and Jalan migrate to the reception counter. The puzzled- yet-amused receptionist gestures Crystal to take a close look at the teens' five intake forms. The receptionist flips through the five questionnaire sheets while reading aloud each of the teens' written responses in the 'Family and Next of Kin' section, "Father: Jalan, Jalan, Jalan, Jalan, Jalan. Mother: Crystal, Crystal, Crystal, Crystal, Crystal. Next of Kin: Uncle Jack, Uncle Jack, Uncle Jack, Uncle Jack, Uncle Jack."

Amused, Crystal grins then turns around to face Shelly, Josie, Cole, Robbie and Micky standing against the lobby wall. The teens notice Crystal looking at them. They flash happy smiles, and in perfect unison, they wave and proudly shout, "Hi Mom !"

...And now that Jack and Crystal have helped pull Jalan and the teens out of the well, maybe, in due time, they too will extend their hands to others trying to climb out of the well.

- TheEnd -

About the Author

Just like the homeless teens within Wet Matches, I too had the odds stacked up against me but I'd never given up as a writer. I was born in rural Spotsylvania County, Virginia on March 12, 1961. Growing up in an impoverished household, my somewhat bleak childhood was made brighter through my desire and efforts to excel in school. Going to school and embracing education was necessary and vital for my growth as a young boy. I'd learned to use my imagination as a distraction from my sometimes dismal surroundings. I'd developed a love for storytelling and writing at a young age, and writing stories became a welcomed and much-needed escape from the periodic, harsh realities of my childhood. After graduating with honors from high school in 1979, I joined the US Air Force and traveled the globe. During my off-duty time, I continued my love of writing. I'm a Quarter-Finals Winner of The Writers Network 14th Annual Screenplay & Fiction Competition of Los Angeles, California. I'm currently residing in Buffalo, New York. I have four daughters (Natasha, Melinda, Randie and Ranielle) and one son Joshua. To learn more about Contemporary American Author Randolph Randy Camp go to http://randy0312. wordpress.com